CONTEMPORARY AMERICAN SUCCESS STORIES

Famous People of Hispanic Heritage

Volume X

Barbara Marvis

Valerie Menard

Christine Granados

Susan Zannos

A Mitchell Lane

Multicultural Biography Series

• Celebrating Diversity •

CONTEMPORARY AMERICAN SUCCESS STORIES
Famous People of Hispanic Heritage

Publisher's Cataloging in Publication
Marvis, Barbara, Valerie Menard, and others.
   Famous people of Hispanic heritage. Vol. X / Barbara Marvis, Valerie Menard and others.
   p. cm. —(Contemporary American success stories)—(A Mitchell Lane
multicultural biography series)
   Includes index.
   LCCN: 95-75963
   ISBN: 1-883845-68-8 (hc)
   ISBN: 1-883845-67-x (pbk)

   1. Hispanic Americans—Biography—Juvenile literature. I. Title.
II. Series.

E184.S75M37 1997
920'.009268

QBI96-20404

Illustrated by Barbara Tidman
Project Editor: Susan R. Scarfe

Mitchell Lane PUBLISHERS

Your Path To Quality Educational Material

P.O. Box 200
Childs, Maryland 21916-0200

TABLE OF CONTENTS

Acknowledgments

Every reasonable effort has been made to gain copyright permission where such permission has been deemed necessary. Any oversight brought to the publisher's attention will be corrected in future printings.

Most of the stories in this series were written through personal interviews and/or with the complete permission of the person, representative of the person, or family of the person being profiled and are authorized biographies. All stories have been thoroughly researched and checked for accuracy, and to the best of our knowledge represent true stories.

We wish to acknowledge with gratitude the generous help of Rebecca Lobo for answering our questions (March 1998) and reviewing our story of her, Kenton Eledin for his help in contacting Ms. Lobo, Bill Richardson and Stuart Nagurka for reviewing our story on Bill Richardson and for their generosity in supplying us with photographs; Linda Chavez-Thompson (telephone interview March 1998) for her help with her story and photographs, and Amy Chavez for allowing us use of her personal photos; and Carlos Mencia (telephone interview February 1998) for his patience and help with photographs and our story of him.

Photograph Credits

The quality of the photographs in this book may vary; many of them are personal snapshots supplied to us courtesy of the person being profiled. Many are very old, one-of-a-kind photos. Most are not professional photographs, nor were they intended to be. The publisher felt that the personal nature of the stories in this book would only be enhanced by real-life, family album–type photos, and chose to include many interesting snapshots, even if they were not quite the best quality. pp. 8, 24, 54, 76 sketches by Barbara Tidman; pp. 16, 19, 21 Allsport; p. 20 AP Photo/Ed Zurga; p. 22 Reuters/Mike Segar/Archive Photos; pp. 27, 28, 29, 30, 31, 32, 33, 34, 38, 41, 42, 43, 46, 48 courtesy Bill Richardson; pp. 57, 58, 60 courtesy Amy Chavez; pp. 63, 69, 72, 73 courtesy Linda Chavez-Thompson; p. 66 AP Photo/Kathy Wilkens; p. 70 AP Photo/Charles Bennett; p. 74 AP Photo/Wilfredo Lee; pp. 79, 80, 83, 85, 91, 94 courtesy Carlos Mencia; pp. 86, 88 courtesy HBO/Janet Van Ham; p. 92 Photo by Ken Pivak courtesy of Galavision.

About the Authors

Barbara Marvis has been a professional writer for nearly twenty years. Motivated by her own experience with ethnic discrimination as a young Jewish girl growing up in suburban Philadelphia, Ms. Marvis developed the **Contemporary American Success Stories** series to dispel racial and ethnic prejudice, to tell culturally diverse stories that maintain ethnic and racial distinction, and to provide positive role models for young minorities. She is the author of several books for young adults, including **Tommy Nuñez: NBA Referee/Taking My Best Shot** and **Selena**. She holds a B.S. degree in English and Communications and an M.Ed. in remedial reading. She specializes in developing books for children that can be read on several reading levels.

Valerie Menard has been an editor for *Hispanic* magazine since the magazine moved to Austin, Texas, in July 1994. Before joining the magazine, she was a managing editor of a bilingual weekly, *La Prensa*. Valerie writes from a Latino perspective and as an advocate for Latino causes. She is the author of several biographies for children including **Oscar De La Hoya** and **Cristina Saralegui**.

Christine Granados is a contributing writer for *Hispanic* magazine and editor of *Moderna*. She has been a journalist and freelance writer for more than 10 years. She has written biographies of Jennifer Lopez, Gigi Fernandez, and Freddy Fender, to name a few.

Susan Zannos has taught at all levels, from preschool to college, in Mexico, Greece, Italy, Russia, and Lithuania, as well as in the United States. She has published a mystery **Trust the Liar** (Walker and Co.) and **Human Types: Essence and the Enneagram** was published by Samuel Weiser in 1997. She has written several books for children, including **Paula Abdul** (Mitchell Lane).

INTRODUCTION

by Kathy Escamilla

One of the fastest growing ethno-linguistic groups in the United States is a group of people who are collectively called Hispanic. The term *Hispanic* is an umbrella term that encompasses people from many nationalities, from all races, and from many social and cultural groups. The label *Hispanic* sometimes obscures the diversity of people who come from different countries and speak different varieties of Spanish. Therefore, it is crucial to know that the term *Hispanic* encompasses persons whose origins are from Spanish-speaking countries, including Spain, Mexico, Central and South America, Cuba, Puerto Rico, the Dominican Republic, and the United States. It is important also to note that Spanish is the heritage language of most Hispanics. However, Hispanics living in the United States are also linguistically diverse. Some speak mostly Spanish and little English, others are bilingual, and some speak only English.

Hispanics are often also collectively called Latinos. In addition to calling themselves Hispanics or Latinos, many people in this group also identify themselves in more specific terms according to their country of origin or their ethnic group (e.g., Cuban-American, Chicano, Puerto Rican-American, etc.). The population of Hispanics in the United States is expected to triple in the next twenty-five years, making it imperative that students in schools understand and appreciate the enormous contributions that persons of Hispanic heritage have made in the Western Hemisphere in general and in the United States in particular.

There are many who believe that in order to be successful in the United States now and in the twenty-first century, all persons from diverse cultural backgrounds, such as Hispanics, should be assimilated. To be assimilated means losing one's distinct cultural and linguistic heritage and changing to or adopting the cultural attributes of the dominant culture.

Others disagree with the assimilationist viewpoint and believe that it is both possible and desirable for persons from diverse cultural backgrounds to maintain their cultural heritage and also to contribute positively and successfully to the dominant culture. This viewpoint is called cultural pluralism, and it is from the perspective of cultural pluralism that these biographies are written. They represent persons who identify strongly with their Hispanic heritage and at the same time who are proud of being citizens of the United States and successful contributors to U.S. society.

The biographies in these books represent the diversity of Hispanic heritage in the United States. Persons featured are contemporary figures whose national origins range from Argentina to Arizona and whose careers and contributions cover many aspects of contemporary life in the United States. These biographies include writers, musicians, actors, journalists, astronauts, businesspeople, judges, political activists, and politicians. Further, they include Hispanic women and men, and thus also characterize the changing role of all women in the United States. Each person profiled in this book is a positive role model, not only for persons of Hispanic heritage, but for any person.

Collectively, these biographies demonstrate the value of cultural pluralism and a view that the future strength of the United States lies in nurturing the diversity of its human potential, not in its uniformity.

Dr. Kathy Escamilla is currently Vice President of the National Association for Bilingual Education and an Associate Professor of Bilingual Education and Multicultural Education at the University of Colorado, Denver. She previously taught at the University of Arizona, and was the Director of Bilingual Education for the Tucson Unified School District in Tucson, Arizona. Dr. Escamilla earned a B.A. degree in Spanish and Literature from the University of Colorado in 1971. Her master's degree is in bilingual education from the University of Kansas, and she earned her doctorate in bilingual education from UCLA in 1987.

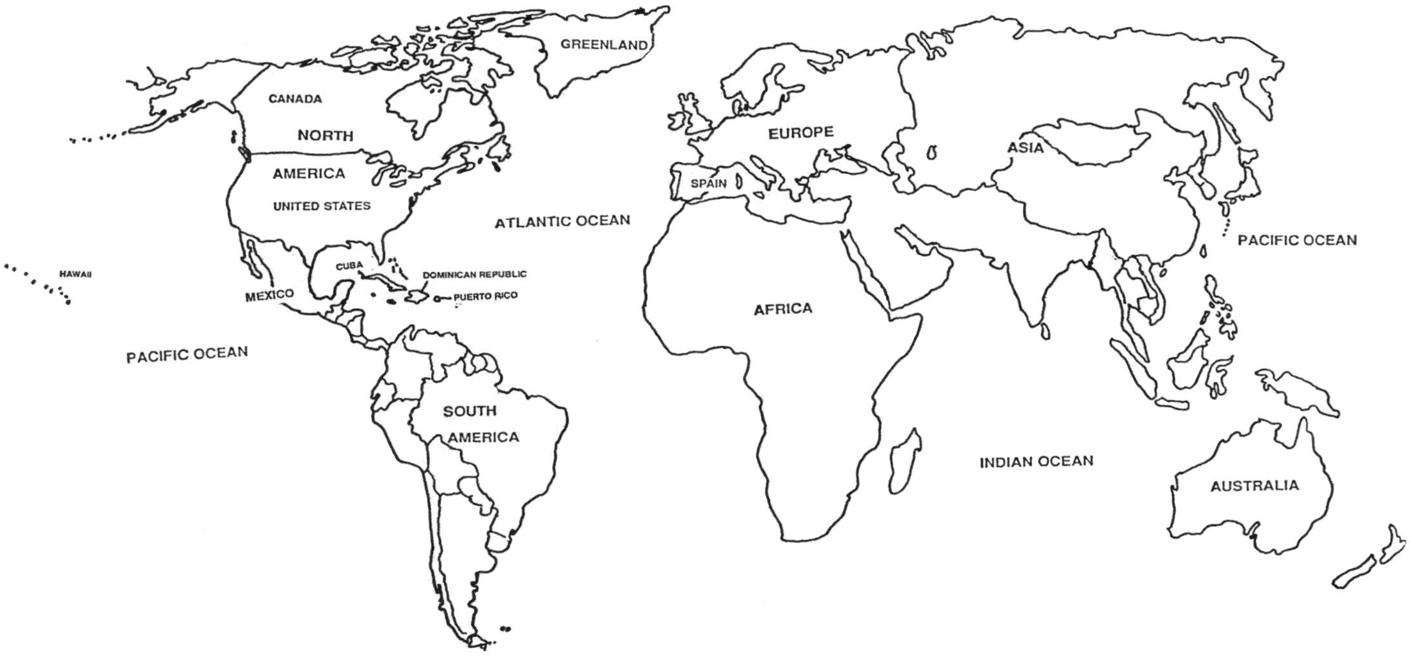

MAP OF THE WORLD

PACIFIC OCEAN

AUSTRALIA

ASIA

INDIAN OCEAN

EUROPE

AFRICA

SPAIN

GREENLAND

ATLANTIC OCEAN

CANADA

NORTH
AMERICA

UNITED STATES

MEXICO

CUBA

DOMINICAN REPUBLIC

PUERTO RICO

SOUTH
AMERICA

PACIFIC OCEAN

HAWAII

REBECCA LOBO

Professional Basketball Player, Television Sports Analyst
1973—

"I am most proud when people compliment the person I have become, because at the end of the day it doesn't matter how many points you can score. What matters is what is in your heart and soul. **"**

-Rebecca Lobo, as told to Christine Granados, March 1998

BIO HIGHLIGHTS

- Born October 6, 1973, in Granby, Connecticut; mother: RuthAnn Lobo; father: Dennis J. Lobo
- 1993-95, selected to the All-Big East first team
- 1994-95, named the Big East Conference Player of the Year, the Big East Tournament Most Outstanding Player, Academic All-America, and the Big East Conference Women's Basketball Scholar Athlete of the Year
- 1995, led UConn to a 35-0 record and the NCAA championship
- 1995, named the Final Four Most Valuable Player, received the Wade Trophy, selected the consensus National Player of the Year and the GTE/CoSIDA Women's Basketball National Academic All-American of the Year, and named to the Associated Press and Kodak All-America first teams
- 1995, graduated from University of Connecticut with a B.A. in political science
- 1996, was the youngest member of the U.S. Women's Olympic Team, which won the gold medal at the Atlanta Games
- January 22, 1997, signed by the WNBA to the New York Liberty
- 1997-98, was a sideline reporter for Connecticut Public Television and an ESPN analyst during the NCAA Tournaments

Rebecca Lobo was the youngest player on the U.S. Women's Basketball Team that won an Olympic gold medal in Atlanta in 1996.

REBECCA LOBO

When 10-year-old Rebecca Lobo had to stand up in front of her entire class to explain why she dressed like a tomboy and why she was the only girl who sat with the boys during lunchtime, she could not. Her teacher scolded her in front of her peers and told her that she needed to change her behavior. Although Rebecca did not agree with her teacher, she said nothing. She merely put her head down on her desk and did not answer or look at her teacher. Rebecca did not let her teacher's beliefs sway or change her mind or personality. She continued to sit with the boys at lunchtime and to dress and act the way she felt most comfortable. It's a good thing too, because as she said in her book, *The Home Team: Of Mothers, Daughters, and American Champions,* if she had listened to her teacher, "I would probably have thought there was something wrong or unfeminine about playing basketball."

And playing basketball is one of the many things Rebecca Lobo does well. Rebecca was the youngest player, 22 at the time, on the U.S. Women's Basketball Team that won the Olympic gold medal at the Atlanta Games in 1996. "It was a great feeling because we worked so hard for it. I don't think I've ever worked harder for anything in my whole life," said Rebecca during an on-line chat. She was chosen to be part of the team because of her successful college basketball career with the University of Connecticut (UConn) Huskies. As a Husky, she made (and still holds) the school's rebounding and blocking records. Rebecca brought down 1,286 rebounds and stuffed 396 shots during her four years in college. She also helped lead UConn to a 35-0 record en route to winning the NCAA championship in 1995. "When you win a championship, at first you simply enjoy the feeling that surrounds you," Rebecca recalled. "The following day, you begin to celebrate what you've done. Then suddenly, the feeling separates from you. It becomes something that happened, something in the past."

Rebecca Lobo was born October 6, 1973, in Granby, Connecticut, to RuthAnn and Dennis Lobo. The family moved to Southwick, Massachusetts, when Rebecca was two years old. Her parents, who are both teachers, still teach in Granby. Rebecca grew up in Southwick, exploring the woods and splashing around in their above-ground swimming pool. She is very close to her brother, Jason, who is six years older than she, and her sister, Rachel, just two years older. The three were always together when they were children because their house was in the country, far from other houses. They grew up stocking a nearby pond with polliwogs and frogs and playing on their Big Wheels and bikes so often that they wore paths through their yard and into the woods.

Like most brothers and sisters, the three were always competing against each other. During the cold winters when they had to play indoors, they focused their attention on board games such as Trivial Pursuit, Boggle, Scrabble, and Trouble. Mom and Dad would play, too. RuthAnn recalls, "Competitive from the start, the kids picked their teams accordingly: Mom for vocabulary and Dad for details." Come summer the three were outdoors again, riding bikes and playing every game imaginable together: stickball, volleyball, wiffle ball, and soccer. Jason told a *Sports Illustrated*

▼▼▼▼▼▼
"When you win a championship, at first you simply enjoy the feeling that surrounds you," Rebecca recalled.
▲▲▲▲▲▲

Rebecca Lobo

writer, "One of my favorite images of Rebecca is her in the homemade catcher's outfit she put together out of paper, with a football helmet on her head, with me pitching and Rachel swinging." Meanwhile, their father, Dennis, taught the children how to shoot hoops. All three became college athletes. Jason played basketball at Dartmouth College, Rachel played at Salem State College, and Rebecca played at UConn.

Dennis Lobo also gave his family their Hispanic heritage. He is of Cuban descent; his father came to the United States from Cuba. "My grandfather was fluent in Spanish, but his sons, including my dad, never learned," said Rebecca. "My grandfather would talk to us a little bit and would speak Spanish occasionally, but we couldn't understand him. My brother can speak Spanish because he spent a semester in Mexico. My sister knows a good amount. She learned from a close Puerto Rican friend. I speak only what I learned in high school. It really is a beautiful language."

Rebecca attended Woodland Elementary School from kindergarten to third grade and Powder Mill School from fourth to eighth grades. She learned her Spanish at Southwick-Tolland Regional High School, where she was a standout on the basketball team. (She scored 2,710 points during her four years there, the most points by any player, girl or boy, in the state's history.) Although the Lobo family did not grow up with an awareness of their Hispanic heritage, Dennis and RuthAnn instilled in their children a strong sense of Christian faith and family. Wherever Rebecca is, her family is not far away. The book Rebecca cowrote with her mother has a chapter written

▼▼▼▼▼▼

Dennis and RuthAnn instilled in their children a strong sense of Christian faith and family.

▲▲▲▲▲▲

by her father, sister, and brother. A constant theme throughout the book is faith and family. "Talking about God sometimes makes others uncomfortable. This is not my intention; God is a presence in my heart and I feel it is important to acknowledge the place He has in my life," Rebecca wrote. Her strong Christian faith has helped her weather many personal storms.

Rebecca's parents are her role models. They always told her that she could be anything she wanted. RuthAnn enforced that belief with action. It was she who insisted that Rebecca be allowed to play on the boys' basketball team. (There weren't enough girls to make up a girls' team in Southwick.) When Rebecca came home the day her teacher told her she acted too much like a boy, her mother's outrage at the incident gave her the support she needed and helped her validate her own identity. It was then that Rebecca knew she was right and her teacher was wrong. She also became more self-confident. "I learned that just because someone is in a position of authority doesn't mean they are always right," said Rebecca.

Rebecca cannot remember a time during her childhood when she was not playing basketball. When and how she started playing remain a mystery. "I simply remember standing in the driveway and shooting for hours at a time," Rebecca explains. "I remember playing alone, playing with my brother and sister, playing with my parents. It was more than a game to me. It was a chance to escape and to dream." That escape would come in handy later in her life.

Not only did she dream while playing basketball, but she also dreamed of playing basketball professionally. When she was eight, she imagined being

▼▼▼▼▼▼
Rebecca's parents are her role models.
▲▲▲▲▲▲

"Now that I'm a few years older and wiser, I realize that I simply cannot play on a men's professional basketball team. But it wasn't easy to convince me of this," says Rebecca.

REBECCA LOBO

the first girl to play for the Boston Celtics. She even went so far as to write Red Auerbach, the general manager of the Celtics at the time, and tell him that when she grew up she would be the first girl to play for his team. "Now that I'm a few years older and wiser, I realize that I simply cannot play on a men's professional basketball team. But it wasn't easy to convince me of this," Rebecca says. She continues:

"I first saw the physical differences between the men's and women's games up close and personal the spring of my sophomore year in college. I was sitting in Gampel Pavilion [the arena where her college basketball team plays home games] after a shooting workout and our men's team was about to play pickup. They had only nine people and asked me if I'd like to join them. . . . As one of my teammates went for a lay-up, I got on the other side of the hoop, in position to get the rebound in case he missed. I never expected him to hang in the air long enough to come over to my side of the basket before shooting. Upon landing, his shoulder went straight into my nose. It started bleeding immediately and I ran to the training room. I didn't start crying until I looked into the mirror and saw a nose shaped like the letter S on my face. I begged the school doctor to make my nose straight again. . . . In the third grade I thought I could compete with the men on that level. Now I realize that I can't. . . ."

All those years of standing in the front yard shooting hoops with her family and practicing in high school won Rebecca a scholarship to the University of Connecticut. "I was nervous when I first entered college," said Rebecca. "I didn't know what to expect from basketball, from classes, or anything else. It was my first time away from home. But I was better off than most because I had my teammates who looked out for me and who took care of me." In college, with the help of her teammates and a lot of hard work, Rebecca blossomed. She received honor after honor at the university, scholastic as well as athletic, where she has broken school and Big East Conference records. (The Big East is the league in which UConn competes in athletic events.)

Rebecca was the most-honored women's basketball player in the nation for her scholar-athlete achievements. She was the only Big East basketball player in history to earn both the Big East Player of the Year and Scholar-Athlete of the Year awards. A political science major, she made the dean's list every semester, and she qualified as a Rhodes Scholar candidate. The award, a two- or three-year scholarship to study at Oxford University in England, is given to 32 American college students with high academic marks. To be a candidate is a great accomplishment.

Rebecca's study habits earned her a nickname at school. "Come exam time, I stressed out and studied as much as I could. I was the sort who read every book on the syllabus [course outline] and attended every class. I was known among the other athletes at school for being a nerd," she said. Her English literature professor Samuel F. Pickering did not consider Rebecca

▼▼▼▼▼▼

"I was nervous when I first entered college," said Rebecca. "I didn't know what to expect."

▲▲▲▲▲▲

a nerd. He was quoted as saying: "I look around the classroom and pick out the people who have sunlight shining from their eyes. Rebecca is one of them." The inner fire Pickering saw is what makes Rebecca such a success on the basketball court as well as in the classroom. This is a woman who compiled a 106-25 win-loss record during her college career and played in four NCAA tournaments.

Rebecca compiled a 106-25 win-loss record during her college career and played in four NCAA tournaments.

Her athletic talent brought her many fans and pushed her into the limelight. Rebecca received sacks of fan mail at UConn, and she diligently replied to every one with a personal letter. "I try to answer every letter I get," she said in a newspaper interview. She also does as many public appearances as she can. At one postgame interview during college, she had to be accompanied by two security guards so as not to be smothered by admiring fans. The celebrity does not bother her. "I have less free time and private time, but I enjoy the opportunity of meeting new people every day," Rebecca said to a fan about the public's demand for her attention.

RuthAnn marveled at her daughter's poise when handling publicity. In *The Home Team,* she describes a scene she witnessed:

"I remember, too, watching Rebecca learn to handle this adoration. There was a young boy, a street kid from Hartford, brought to a game by his social worker. When I introduced him to Rebecca after the game, he was speechless, paralyzed with awe. 'Come over here,' she said. Putting her arm around his shoulder, she asked about his interests. When he offered a quiet question, she whispered an answer in his ear. He continued to simply gaze at her. It was obvious he felt like the most important person in Gampel Pavilion. I witnessed this and scenes similar to it repeatedly. To see my daughter, not long out of childhood herself, reach out to a young boy and identify his worth as a human being was a scene I will always keep in my heart."

Rebecca's celebrity gave her the opportunity to jog alongside the President of the United States, Bill Clinton. "I ran behind the president for the first one and a half miles, with the fear of catching his legs and tripping him," Rebecca said. After the three-mile jog the president took Rebecca, her brother, Jason, and a friend on a personal tour of the Oval Office.

In 1993, the entire Lobo family was thrust into the spotlight the night Rebecca accepted her award for Big East Player of the Year. Rebecca thanked God, her coaches, and her teammates, then said the award was for her mother, "who is the real competitor this year." That was the night Rebecca decided to tell the public that her mother, RuthAnn, had been diagnosed with breast cancer. Newspaper, television, and magazine reporters telephoned the family for interviews after Rebecca's speech. "I'll never forget her courage the day she told me about the results of her biopsy," Rebecca

▼▼▼▼▼▼

"I ran behind the president for the first one and a half miles, with the fear of catching his legs and tripping him," Rebecca said.

▲▲▲▲▲▲

said about her mother. "She pulled me aside following the game against Virginia my junior year and informed me that a lump was found in her breast and that the lump was malignant. Here I was a woman who had just played one of the best games of her career and competed in one of her team's biggest victories. It seemed to me that the wrong woman was crying. . . . The woman who was the strength, the comforter, the giver of life, was the mother. The woman who needed strength, comfort, and life, was the daughter."

Rebecca buried herself in her studies during her junior year of college. She worked hard in practice and used the basketball court to escape from the fact that she might lose her mother to cancer. "Basketball was what saved me during that time. . . . Practicing or playing was the only time I could completely free my mind of everything that was going on; . . . my mom's illness would not enter my mind at all as long as I was on the court playing this simple game."

RuthAnn made it a point to stand tough during this turbulent time. Despite surgery to remove the cancerous lump in her breast and chemotherapy treatments that made her sick, RuthAnn resolved to attend every one of Rebecca's home games. "I arranged my treatments around the UConn women's basketball schedule. I was determined not miss a game," said RuthAnn. "Rebecca's basketball games took on new meaning for me. Not only were they benchmarks around which I scheduled my treatments, they were something to look forward to. I was determined not to worry my daughter by my absence at a game."

RuthAnn remembered during that time how many people would come up to her at basketball games

▼▼▼▼▼▼

Despite her illness, RuthAnn resolved to attend every one of Rebecca's games.

▲▲▲▲▲▲

and share their horror stories of cancer. These encounters prompted her and Rebecca to write *The Home Team*. "It was humbling to be the recipient of so much personal and heartrending disclosure. After a time, I stopped asking why. If someone found solace in talking to me, I made myself available to listen. It was an honor," said RuthAnn.

By the time Rebecca graduated from college, her mother was cancer free. Rebecca continued to forge ahead and pave a path for women in basketball. She had planned to play professional basketball in Europe for a few years, then return to the United States to attend law school— that is, until the Women's National Basketball Association came calling. David Stern, the commissioner of the National Basketball Association, recognized the popularity of women's basketball in 1996 when the National Team, of which Rebecca was a member, won the Olympic gold medal. Stern decided to try his luck at a professional women's league. "I never really thought there would be one during my career," said Rebecca. "No one could foresee the explosion of interest in women's basketball that [has] occurred. . ."

Rebecca played in the 1996 Olympic Games in Atlanta, Georgia. The photograph below was taken in July 1996 during the game against Japan.

REBECCA LOBO

Rebecca was one of the first players to sign up with the WNBA and play for the New York Liberty.

In the league's first season Rebecca was named to the All-WNBA second team. She did not expect so much fan support in the league's first season. "The thing that has pleasantly surprised me has been the fan

In 1995, Rebecca was named Woman of the Year by the NCAA. Here she is answering a reporter's question during a news conference before the NCAA dinner, which celebrated her accomplishments in leading UConn to an undefeated season.

turnout. The fans have not only come out in large numbers, but they've been *great* fans. Especially on the road—they've cheered for the good plays, no booing or negative things coming from the stands, and they've stayed to the end of the game no matter what the score. They've rallied behind their teams and I've really been excited about that," said Rebecca. Her New York team made it to the first ever WNBA championship finals, where they ultimately lost to the Houston Comets.

REBECCA LOBO

The six-foot four-inch center is one of the WNBA's better-known players. She was a guest on *The Late Show with David Letterman,* as well as on *Live! with Regis and Kathie Lee, The Rosie O'Donnell Show, Good Morning America, CBS This Morning,* and many others. She made a guest appearance on the sitcom *Mad About You* in 1997 and got to play one-on-one with Big Bird on *Sesame Street* in 1998. "Being on Letterman was something I never imagined," Rebecca told Mary Duffy in an interview for *Women's Sports Fitness Magazine.* In a live on-line chat, Rebecca told cyber junkies that she enjoyed her guest appearance on *Mad About You* and wants to continue to do guest appearances on television. Because of her presence on television and the screen, Rebecca landed a cameo role in the Oscar-nominated film *Jerry Maguire,* which starred Tom Cruise. However, her scene did not make the final version of the movie. Rebecca's stint as an ESPN analyst during the 1997 and the 1998 NCAA Tournaments has assured her a spot on television, even if no sitcoms come calling.

Rebecca scores for New York Liberty during the Great Western Forum played in Inglewood, California.

REBECCA LOBO

Rebecca also contributes her time and efforts to charities. She became the national spokesperson for the Lee National Denim Day, sponsored by Lee Apparel Company, whose goal was to raise $1 million for the Susan G. Komen Foundation. The foundation is dedicated to breast cancer research. She is also part of the Children's Miracle Network Champions, which has helped raise money for children's hospitals around the United States and for the Pediatric AIDS Foundation. She received the Most Caring Athlete Award from *USA Weekend* magazine in 1997 for her commitment to helping others.

Just like professional men's basketball players such as Michael Jordan and Shaquille O'Neal, Rebecca has numerous company endorsement contracts. She can be seen in advertisements for Reebok International, Ltd., Spalding Sports Worldwide, General Motors Corporation's Buick Division, Fleet Services Corporation, Huffy Sports, and Sears, Roebuck and Company. After just one year, professional women's basketball had become a marketable game, allowing the players to endorse products and earn large paychecks. Rebecca is quick to add, "I don't want to see basketball lose its true meaning for women in the rush of endorsement contracts, although the contracts are long overdue. I don't want to see women's basketball lose its meaning for those fans who were there before the sneaker companies were. It's up to the

Rebecca holds her "ESPY" award after being named top athlete for 1995 at the ESPN "ESPY" awards ceremony at Radio City Music Hall, February 13, 1996.

players to keep the innocence we have in our game. . . . We must be responsible."

Rebecca is already making plans for her future. She wants to turn the ESPN sports analyst position into a full-time career. "After I'm done playing basketball, which hopefully won't be for at least another ten years, I do plan on pursuing a broadcasting career," Rebecca said. "I also have a dream of having a family of my own someday." Rebecca Lobo understands what makes a person truly successful: love of family and character. Those are the values her family instilled in her from the beginning, and those are the same values that have made the record-breaking basketball star so popular. Of all her hundreds of accomplishments, Rebecca says she is honored most when people admire her character. "I am most proud when people compliment the person I have become, because at the end of the day it doesn't matter how many points you can score. What matters is what is in your heart and soul."

The young tomboy of Southwick has come a long way from the time she was humiliated in front of her classmates. Her many successes and the stance she decided to take during that defining moment in her life have helped to change attitudes nationwide. Gone are the days when women in the United States have to play basketball in other countries. Young girls no longer have to dream of playing in men's leagues, and women athletes are considered feminine and beautiful. . . . thanks in large part to Rebecca Lobo.

Rebecca is already making plans for her future. She wants to turn the ESPN sports analyst position into a full-time career.

24

BILL RICHARDSON

Congressman, U.N. Ambassador, Secretary of Energy
1947–

"If there's one word that comes to mind when I think of Bill Richardson, it really is energy. **"**

—President Bill Clinton, August 18, 1998, as Bill Richardson was sworn in as the ninth United States Secretary of Energy

---

BIO HIGHLIGHTS

- Born on November 15, 1947, in Pasadena, California; mother: Maria Luisa Lopez-Collada; father: William Richardson
- Lived in Mexico City from 1947 to 1963
- Attended boarding school in New England, 1963–1966
- 1966, drafted by the Kansas City Athletics to play professional baseball but attended college instead
- 1970, earned B.A. degree in political science and French from Tufts University
- 1971, earned M.A. degree from Fletcher School of Law and Diplomacy
- 1972, married Barbara Flavin
- 1974–1976, employed by U.S. State Department
- 1976–1978, aide to the Senate Foreign Affairs Committee
- 1978–1982, businessman and director of Democratic Party in New Mexico
- 1983–1997, congressman from Third Congressional District, New Mexico
- February 1994, visited Aung San Suu Kyi in Burmese prison in February; met with Raoul Cedras in Haiti for return of democracy in July; negotiated release of Bobby Hall in North Korea in December
- August 1995, negotiated with Saddam Hussein to free engineers in August; nominated for Nobel Peace Prize
- 1997, nominated for the Nobel Peace Prize
- 1996, negotiated release of three Red Cross workers in Sudan on December 8; appointed U.S. Ambassador to United Nations on December 13
- Appointment confirmed by U.S. Senate on February 10, 1997
- June 18, 1998, appointed U.S. Secretary of Energy by President Clinton, confirmed by Senate on July 31, sworn in on August 18.

Guerrilla commander Kerubino Kwanyin Bol waited in the village while his men escorted Congressman Bill Richardson to a table under a mango tree where negotiations would take place.

BILL RICHARDSON

The plane landed on the dirt runway of an airfield near the Sudanese village of Gogrial. Armed rebel soldiers wearing camouflage uniforms and carrying assault rifles lined up, watching as a rumpled figure in a blue blazer emerged from the plane. Guerrilla commander Kerubino Kwanyin Bol waited in the village while his men escorted Congressman Bill Richardson to a table under a mango tree where negotiations would take place.

Taking part in the negotiations with Richardson and Kerubino was Sudan's ambassador to the United States, Mahdi I. Mohamed. For four hours the men attempted to reach an agreement that would free three Red Cross workers—pilot John Early from New Mexico, his Kenyan copilot Moshen Raza, and Australian nurse Mary Worthington—who had been captured and imprisoned by the rebel forces over a month before. The three had been transporting wounded soldiers when they were seized by Kerubino's men.

Kerubino was demanding $2.5 million for the release of the prisoners. Richardson, the congressman from New Mexico's Third Congressional District, repeated the International Committee of the Red Cross's offer of five tons of rice, four jeeps, and nine radios. The negotiating parties seemed impossibly far apart. When they took a break to stretch their legs, Richardson walked over to one of the village huts. Inside, Kerubino's daughter lay ill with a virulent form of measles, which had claimed the life of her sister the previous day. Richardson visited the sick child briefly before returning to the negotiating table.

BILL RICHARDSON

The rebel leader was obviously moved by this simple demonstration of compassion. As Kerubino spoke, Richardson listened. Richardson added to the offer a complete health survey of the rebel camp; much-needed medical assistance, including vaccines for the village children; and help in cleaning up the local water supply. Finally Kerubino asked for a tractor in addition to the supplies and services already offered. Richardson agreed. A few hours later the three Red Cross workers had been released and were on a plane headed home.

How did it happen that a congressman from New Mexico was able to reach the heart and mind of one of the fiercest and most determined rebel leaders

In December 1996, Congressman Bill Richardson (seated second from right) negotiates the release of three International Red Cross workers with rebel leader Kerubino (center, seated with hat).

BILL RICHARDSON

of Africa? How was he able to bridge the enormous gap of different languages and different cultures in order to arrive at an agreement that benefitted them both? As Rogelio Novey, a friend and former classmate of Richardson, said, "Remember, he's been trained in this international business his whole life."

Bill Richardson's father, William Richardson, was an executive of First National City Bank, now Citibank, the only U.S. bank permitted to operate in Mexico. His mother, Maria Luisa Lopez-Collada, was Mexican. After the couple married, they established their home in Mexico City. On November 15, 1947,

Bill's athletic ability was apparent even as a toddler.

their son, Bill Richardson, was born in Pasadena, California; however, he spent his childhood in Mexico City. Bill's sister, Vesta, who is now a doctor practicing in Mexico, was born in 1956. The children were completely bilingual from infancy, speaking both Spanish and English.

Later, the transition from his childhood in the warm, emotional culture of Mexico to boarding school in the more cool and practical culture of New England was a shock for Bill. But he soon bridged the gap between the two cultures with his genial friendliness, his aptitude for foreign languages (he particularly excelled in French), and his love of sports. He won the admiration of his classmates with his athletic ability, particularly when his strong pitching arm led the baseball team to the championship.

Bill's ball playing was good enough to attract the attention of scouts from the Kansas City Athletics, who drafted him in 1966. At that time, baseball was the most important thing in his life. But his father wanted him to go to college. Choosing between college and major-league baseball was the hardest decision he'd ever had to make. Finally, he did as his father wished.

Bill enrolled in Tufts University, the college his father had attended. It turned out to be the right

Bill, right, with sister, Vesta in 1956

BILL RICHARDSON

AMERICAN SOCIETY OF MEXICO
BULLETIN

As a young boy, Bill's interest in international affairs was beginning.

decision: the following year his elbow went out and he was no longer able to pitch. (He remained an enthusiastic ballplayer, however, later playing third base for the Democrats' team in the House of Representatives.) At Tufts, Bill Richardson's interest was drawn to classes in international affairs. He graduated in 1970 with a double major in political science and French.

The following year, he earned a master's degree from Tufts' Fletcher School of Law and Diplomacy.

BILL RICHARDSON

In 1972, Bill Richardson married Barbara Flavin, a girl he had met when he was a teenager; she had picked him up while he was hitchhiking. Also that year his father died.

In 1974, the young Bill Richardson got a job as an assistant in the Congressional Relations Office of the State Department. His decision to work for the

Bill and his mother

BILL RICHARDSON

Bill as a teenager

State Department was inspired by an experience he had while still in school. On a field trip to visit the Senate, he had heard Senator Hubert Humphrey giving an impassioned speech about Africa. Both moved and impressed, Richardson knew that he wanted to be a part of the international world that Humphrey described. After two years at the State Department, he went to work as an aide for the Senate Foreign Relations Committee. He worked for the man who had inspired him, Senator Hubert Humphrey.

What Bill Richardson learned during those years was that one man could make a difference. The efforts of one person could affect the course of history and change the lives of many people. Richardson wanted to be a person who made a difference, a person who put his abilities and knowledge and efforts to work to make situations in the world better. He realized that he would be in a much better position to make a difference if he held an elected office, as Senator Humphrey and the others on the Foreign Relations Committee did. In order to realize his goals, Bill Richardson had to make long-term plans, and he had to have the courage to follow them through even when it seemed as if he might fail.

In order to put his plans into effect, he had to leave his job in Washington, D.C.

Bill Richardson chose to live in New Mexico after visiting there several times. He and his wife, Barbara, moved there in 1978, and he became a businessman active in the Hispanic community and in the chamber of commerce. He accepted the position of executive director of the Democratic Party of the state. His political enemies accused him of being a carpetbagger (someone who moves to an area only to exploit it, as occurred in the Southern states after the Civil War), but Bill Richardson was deeply concerned and involved with the citizens of New Mexico and the issues that faced them.

Bill with wife, Barbara during his first run for Congress in 1980.

In 1980, Richardson entered the race for the congressional seat held by Republican representative Manuel Lujan, Jr., who didn't think Richardson had a chance. To Lujan's surprise—and to many others'—Richardson conducted such an active campaign that he came to within 1 percent of winning. Although he didn't win the election, Richardson won a place in the *Guinness Book of World Records* for shaking 8,871 hands. Clearly this was a man who was serious about achieving his goals.

BILL RICHARDSON

Two years later, in 1982, Richardson entered the contest to be elected to the House of Representatives from the newly created Third Congressional District of New Mexico. This district covered the northern part of the state and included the tourist centers of Santa Fe and Taos, the largest community of Sikhs (a religious group from India) in the United States, the Los Alamos nuclear labs, cattle ranches, 18 separate American Indian tribes, and a population that was 34 percent Hispanic. If ever a congressional district needed a representative who was sensitive to cultural differences, it was this one. And the people recognized that Bill Richardson was the man they needed to represent them.

Speaking at a Capitol Hill news conference

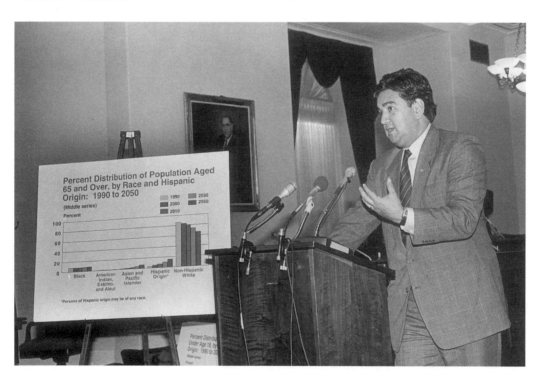

BILL RICHARDSON

Richardson not only won that first election by a wide margin, but he was returned to office every two years for the next six elections. He won every reelection by 60 percent or more, serving from January of 1983 until he was sworn in as United States Ambassador to the United Nations in February of 1997. During his fourteen years in the House of Representatives, Bill Richardson had plenty of opportunities to develop his skills of negotiating and of representing different interest groups.

Like any new member of the House of Representatives, Congressman Richardson had to learn to get along in two different organizations. One was the House itself, with the different committees that do the actual work of preparing legislation. The other was the political party to which he belonged, the Democratic Party. In both arenas, his ability to get along well with others and to understand them, to listen and find out what made them tick, served him well.

The real work of the House of Representatives is done in committees. It is impossible for all members of the House to be completely informed on all the issues, so representatives specialize in different areas and keep their colleagues informed. Bill Richardson served on the Resources and Commerce Committees in the House of Representatives, and on the Select Intelligence Committee, which is the counterpart of the Senate Foreign Affairs Committee. He became a senior member of the Select Intelligence Committee, and it was in this capacity that he began taking many fact-finding missions to trouble spots around the globe.

From the time he won his first election, Bill Richardson was returned to office every two years for the next six elections.

BILL RICHARDSON

In the structure of the Democratic Party within the House of Representatives, Richardson rose to the position of chief deputy whip. The party whips are the people responsible for keeping track of the position of each party member on a particular piece of legislation. If the whip learns that a congressman is undecided, then he or she will try to influence that person to vote along party lines. In other words, this too is a position in which patience and the ability to negotiate and persuade are required. Richardson also served a term as chairman of the congressional Hispanic caucus, and was effective in supporting legislation that was in the best interests of the Hispanic community.

But it wasn't only in Washington, D.C., that Richardson's ability to resolve the differences between different factions was called upon. At home in New Mexico, he was able to gain the continuing support of the many different interest groups he represented. He didn't try to be all things to all people. He was too active and too honest for that. Whenever his vote displeased some of his constituents, he would meet with the voters in person to explain why he had taken the position he had. Bill Richardson held more than two thousand town meetings to keep the people of New Mexico informed about how he was voting and why. The people may not always have agreed with him, but they were impressed both by his honesty and by the hard work he did on their behalf.

Even though his position on specific issues was not always popular, Richardson voted according to his best understanding and his own conscience, even when that went against the prevailing vote of the Democratic Party. In 1994 he was instrumental in the passage of

▼▼▼▼▼▼
He didn't try to be all things to all people.
▲▲▲▲▲▲

NAFTA, the North American Free Trade Agreement, and was the only member of the House Democratic leadership to support and lobby for it. Richardson felt that trade between Mexico and New Mexico would increase, and that his home state would greatly benefit from the huge market in Mexico. He urged the governor of New Mexico and other government officials and businessmen to travel to Mexico frequently and to develop an understanding of the ways in which closer economic and cultural ties would be to their mutual advantage.

Richardson emphasized the need for understanding between cultures that is the foundation of his success in negotiations: "In negotiating and dealing between countries, establishing cultural and social ties is very important. Latin American societies are more personal than European societies. They don't want to just cut a deal by fax or by cellular phone. They want to see you, they want to have a meal with you, they want to get a sense of your being. And that requires a lot of time. But I think that if it pays off in some significant investment on both sides, it's worth it." Richardson added that he knows all the Mexican leaders personally and would be glad to accompany U.S. officials to Mexico.

In addition to smoothing situations in Congress that required conciliation rather than confrontation, and to explaining his voting record to his constituents without alienating those who did not agree with him, Bill Richardson was frequently called upon to negotiate between factions within the state of New Mexico. The separate and sovereign Indian Nations frequently were involved in disputes about land use and economic

▼▼▼▼▼

"In negotiating and dealing between countries, establishing cultural and social ties is very important," says Bill.

▲▲▲▲▲▲

conditions on their reservations. Each tribe had its own language and culture; each had its own problems and conflicts. Richardson needed to understand them all in order to work in their best interests.

Richardson's work on the Resources Committee was of use in the varied problems facing Indian tribes. He was critical of the Bureau of Indian Affairs, calling it "a very inefficient bureaucracy that not only misadministers existing programs for Indians but is ineffective in . . . investing Indian trust funds from

From left to right: President Bill Clinton, Speaker Thomas Foley, and Congressman Bill Richardson (1993)

federal lands." He called for reinvigorating the BIA and favored the self-government of Native Americans. Richardson felt that the gaming issue—building gambling casinos on Indian land—was causing the Indians to "get hooked on the gaming dollars." He felt this approach to economic development was preventing the tribes from developing other types of businesses. Specifically he thought there needed to be ways for the Indians to profit from the tourist dollars that they were instrumental in bringing to New Mexico.

During his first six terms as the representative from the Third Congressional District of New Mexico, the Democrats were the majority party in the House of Representatives. Because of his position of seniority on committees and his high position in the party, it was possible for Richardson to be an effective legislator. He was instrumental in getting many important laws passed. But in 1994 the Republicans won the majority of seats in the House, and it was more difficult for the Democrats to get the votes they needed. This was a frustrating period for them, but the result was that Richardson's abilities to negotiate, persuade, and convince found another, larger arena in which to work.

As a senior member of the Select Intelligence Committee, Bill Richardson was aware of the many problem areas in foreign affairs. He was called upon to make fact-finding trips to various trouble spots around the world. Since he was not on official diplomatic missions, he did not have the entire force of the United States government and military behind him: he was just a congressman with an overnight bag gathering information for his committee. It was

▼▼▼▼▼▼

During his first six terms in the House, the Democrats were the majority party.

▲▲▲▲▲▲

possible for Richardson to travel to different parts of the world and deal with hostile dictators and difficult situations in governments that the U.S. administration did not officially recognize. On the other hand, the people with whom Richardson spoke were well aware that he would be reporting to the president of the most powerful nation in the world.

About his negotiating techniques, Richardson said, "Just building in the minds of some of these dictators that they'll have somebody to talk to that they can trust is helpful. I let these governments, especially unfriendly ones, know I can pass messages. They know I'm going to end up talking to the White House. There's now the perception that the United States is the only superpower out there. Any entity associated with the U.S. government automatically has a leg up."

Richardson's first widely publicized trip for the House Intelligence Committee took place in February of 1994 when he visited Burma. He was the first non-family member allowed to visit Nobel Peace Prize-winner Aung San Suu Kyi, leader of the Burmese democracy movement. She had been held under house arrest by the repressive military government in Burma for more than four years. When she was allowed to break her long silence to speak with Congressman Richardson, this brave champion of human rights seemed to enjoy their conversation. They covered other topics than that of her imprisonment and the Burmese political situation. Richardson said later that she was a Michael Jordan fan and asked him if he thought the basketball player would succeed as a baseball player. They made a bet. She bet that Jordan would do well in baseball and Richardson bet against it.

Richardson's first widely publicized trip for the House Intelligence Committee took place in February of 1994 when he visited Burma.

BILL RICHARDSON

This casual, personal style, the ability to make direct human connections with people in the midst of tense, politically dangerous conditions, is a major factor in Richardson's success in defusing explosive situations. He listens to people and learns what their interests and enthusiasms are. This makes him sometimes far more effective than the professional diplomats who arrive surrounded with official assistants and military attachés. It has also sometimes baffled and infuriated those of his opponents who believe that everything has to be done through official channels. They sometimes accuse him of grandstanding, of using such encounters as his talk with Aung San Suu Kyi for his own political advantage. He was also criticized for talking with the Burmese junta and listening to their views. The fact

In February 1994, Congressman Bill Richardson met with Burmese Political dissident Aung San Suu Kyi who was under house arrest.

remains, however, that Congressman Richardson achieved his goal in Burma: a few months later Aung San Suu Kyi was freed and was no longer under house arrest.

Later in 1994, in July, Bill Richardson went to Haiti to talk with military leader Raoul Cedras, who had seized power in a military coup. Richardson had learned, before going to Haiti, that Cedras and one of his generals, Philippe Biamby, liked to play good cop–bad cop, with Biamby doing the threatening. At one point during the meeting, Biamby jumped up and began screaming that he didn't like the U.S. calling him a thug. Richardson calmly turned to Cedras and said, "I don't think he likes me very much." Cedras laughed and said, "All right, Biamby, sit down."

In July 1994, Bill Richardson met with Haiti General Raoul Cedras (center) and his advisers.

BILL RICHARDSON

Able to speak with Cedras and his generals in French without interpreters, Richardson joined them for a five-hour dinner meeting. His mission was to convince the unwilling Cedras that the Congress and the American people would back President Clinton's effort to restore democracy. The result of their long discussion was that Cedras eventually agreed to step down as military ruler to clear the way for the reinstatement of Jean-Bertrand Aristide, the democratically elected president of Haiti. A Washington lawyer who accompanied Richardson to Haiti said, "He's a real asset to the United States. . . . He doesn't travel with an entourage and he's not obsequious. He sits eye to eye and really tries to understand their point of view. There was no Lone Ranger approach."

In December 1994, Bill Richardson arrived in North Korea to talk about enforcing their agreement to stop developing nuclear weapons. Just as he arrived, it was learned that an American helicopter had crashed in North Korean territory. One of the pilots had been killed in the crash and the other, Bobby Hall, had been captured. Richardson immediately began negotiating for the release of Hall and the return of the body of the dead pilot. As always,

January 1995—Bill Richardson with Chief Warrant Officer Bobby Hall and his wife, Donna

BILL RICHARDSON

when Richardson undertakes such negotiations, he did not rely on his own opinions but remained in close contact with the State Department. He ran up a $10,000 telephone bill as he received constant directions from the Secretary of State during the five long days of negotiations. Richardson was successful in obtaining both the release of Bobby Hall and the body of his copilot.

Because of his reliability in following instructions from the White House and from the State Department, Bill Richardson was called upon more and more for difficult missions during the next two years. When preparing for a meeting, Richardson would begin by learning everything he could about the person with whom he would be negotiating. He would read all the available biographical material; talk to journalists, scholars, and State Department experts; and consult with people who knew the person. Before meeting with Saddam Hussein in August 1995, Richardson talked with Iraq's ambassador to the United Nations about the Iraqi dictator. He got the advice to be very honest with Hussein.

Even with all the preparation possible, things still sometimes go wrong. Richardson tells that at the beginning of his meeting with Saddam Hussein, the Iraqi president suddenly became angry and left the room. When the baffled Richardson asked what had happened, he was told that he had crossed his leg and revealed the sole of his shoe, which is considered a very great insult in Arab cultures. The interpreter told Richardson that Hussein would return to the meeting and that Richardson should apologize. Richardson, however, did not apologize. He said simply, "Mr.

Because of his reliability in following instructions from the White House and the State Department, Bill Richardson was called upon more and more.

President, let me continue." He knew it was a gamble, but he felt that it was important not to show weakness in the situation.

Richardson was in Baghdad to persuade Hussein to release two American engineers who had mistakenly driven their jeep into Iraq from Kuwait and had been captured. By the time Richardson arrived, David Daliberti and Bill Barloon had been in jail for 114 days. By the end of the 90 minutes of negotiations, Hussein had freed the two engineers and had invited Richardson to visit again. The Iraqi president liked the Acoma Pueblo pottery Richardson had brought from New Mexico. More important, Hussein was hoping that the United Nations embargo against Iraq would be lifted. In that meeting, however, the release of the two engineers was the only topic under discussion.

Richardson says that when he is negotiating for the release of hostages, the prisoners are his only concern. He makes it clear to the other side that they are not there to resolve the differences between their countries. He has a clear goal and relentlessly comes back to it again and again, using every technique he has ever developed: blustering, being respectful, joking, finding mutual areas of interest, and always refocusing on the original aim. He also appeals to the leader's advisers, trying to get them to help. In Iraq he appealed to Hussein's deputy prime minister, Tariq Aziz, emphasizing that they were both Roman Catholics. When the Americans had been released, Richardson attended mass with Aziz's wife.

When Richardson went to Cuba in 1996 to talk to Castro about the release of political prisoners, he spoke first with vice president Carlos Lage and

Richardson says that when he is negotiating for the release of hostages, the prisoners are his only concern.

BILL RICHARDSON

established a connection with him. Later, during negotiations with Castro, Richardson turned to Lage and said, "Come on, help me out, will you?" By this strategy he was able to keep the conversation alive and Castro finally agreed to release three dissidents who were in prison. Richardson also won the freedom of the families of the prisoners. He and Castro sat up late one night talking in Spanish about baseball, American politics, and a wide range of subjects both men were interested in.

In February 1996, Richardson returned to Miami with three political prisoners from Cuba. To Richardson's left is freed political prisoner Carmen Arias Iglesias.

In this instance as in others, Richardson's achievements did not meet with universal approval. Another member of the Hispanic caucus in the House of Representatives, Republican Representative Lincoln

Diaz-Balart of Florida, accused Richardson of acting on behalf of the Clinton administration when he tried to stop the creation of an international embargo against Cuba. Richardson denied this, saying his main concern was with human rights and the freeing of political prisoners.

Richardson was no comic book superhero appearing unbidden at the scene of a crime. If he was not on a specific mission financed and requested by the Select Intelligence Committee of the House of Representatives, he would not enter into a negotiation—unless the family of a hostage, the State Department, and the country holding the hostage all invited him to do so. This occurred on several occasions. When Albuquerque residents Joseph and Jamie Rivera were returning from their South Pacific honeymoon, protesters in Tahiti mobbed their airplane. The couple returned to their hotel and called relatives, and the relatives called the offices of their representatives. Richardson took the initiative in calling the U.S. State Department and the French government, which governs Tahiti, and in 24 hours the newlyweds were on their way home.

Soon afterward Richardson was headed back to North Korea to arrange the release of Evan Hunziker, who had been captured when he mistakenly swam into North Korean waters. He was accused of being a spy and had been imprisoned for three months. Richardson had scarcely returned from that trip when he received a call, on December 1, 1996, from Albuquerque resident Sherry Early. Her husband, a pilot for the Red Cross, had been captured by rebel leader Kerubino's soldiers in the Sudan. She begged

Richardson headed to North Korea to arrange the release of Evan Hunziker who had been captured when he mistakenly swam into North Korean waters.

BILL RICHARDSON

Congressman Richardson to help free her husband. A week later Richardson was on his way to the Sudan, where he met with Kerubino and was successful in getting Early and the other Red Cross workers released.

On December 13 of that year, President Bill Clinton announced that Bill Richardson was his choice for a cabinet position: the United States Ambassador to the United Nations. President Clinton said, "All Americans have watched admiringly as Bill Richardson has undertaken the toughest and most delicate diplomatic efforts around the world." On February 10, 1997, Richardson's appointment was confirmed by the Senate. Later that same month, Bill and Barbara Richardson moved into the official ambassador's residence in the Waldorf Towers in New York City.

March 1997— Ambassador Richardson casts a veto in the UN Security Council.

BILL RICHARDSON

Ambassador Richardson arrived in New York at a time when the relationship between the United States and the United Nations was particularly difficult. Probably the main source of friction was the United States' debt to the United Nations of more than $1 billion in back dues. This, as British Ambassador John Weston observed, "poisons the working environment." The position of the U.S. Congress was that the U.N. ought to be organized more efficiently and to cut down on administrative expenses; only then would the United States pay the money owed. Richardson made solving this dilemma his top priority. He has been speaking with his former colleagues in Congress in an attempt to gain support for a bill that would authorize payment of the dues.

On a much smaller scale, Richardson has mediated in the daily frustrations and antagonisms that have occurred between the emissaries from the nations of the world and the law enforcement agencies of New York City. A major source of conflict is the parking situation in Manhattan. The diplomats representing the member states of the United Nations had run up $6 million worth of traffic fines because of a shortage of parking spaces. Richardson was able to work with the city and member states to foster communication and alleviate the problem.

From one angle Richardson's role as ambassador was similar to that of unofficial negotiator for the Select Intelligence Committee. But from another point of view his situation was now much different. Where before he did not have the entire weight of United States Foreign Policy behind him, now he did. When he was negotiating for the release of hostages or for the

Ambassador Richardson arrived in New York at a time when the relationship between the United States and the United Nations was particularly difficult.

BILL RICHARDSON

freedom of human rights activists who had been imprisoned by repressive governments, he had very clearly defined aims and was not concerned with the relationship between nations. As ambassador he was very much concerned with that relationship, since his goal was to advance U.S. foreign policy interests, particularly, as he phrased it, in "peace, democracy, open markets, human rights, and sustainable development." Instead of going into negotiations with a clear aim and obstinately sitting for several hours until he reached it, he now had to consult constantly with the U.S. State Department, with the President of the United States, with the Secretary General of the United Nations, and with the other ambassadors from other countries.

Richardson no longer traveled light, simply grabbing the overnight bag he kept in his Capitol Hill office and taking off for the other side of the world. Now he had to travel with full diplomatic escort in a chauffeured limousine to specially chartered flights. His informal, open, friendly style of communicating was tailored to the formalities and official protocol of international relations. Nonetheless, the relationships he formed, the close human connections and understandings he made all over the world, created a foundation for his work with the United Nations.

As ambassador, Richardson made several more trips to Africa. One of his first assignments was to Zaire, where he successfully arranged a meeting between the dictator Mobutu Sese Seko and rebel leader Laurent Kabila, who controlled most of the country. He also worked to smooth the way for President Clinton's first official visit to Africa.

▼▼▼▼▼▼

As ambassador, Richardson made several more trips to Africa.

▲▲▲▲▲▲

BILL RICHARDSON

And Richardson has been back to Haiti. In July 1997 he visited Haiti as the United States Ambassador to the United Nations, almost exactly three years after the five-hour-long dinner in which he persuaded Raoul Cedras to step down. The island had been in turmoil since the re-establishment of the elected government in 1994. Their police recruits were inexperienced and frequently too violent. The 1,300 United Nations troops and 225 civilian police monitors were trying to stabilize the political situation and protect human rights there. Richardson, who was thoroughly familiar with the situation, urged a longer period of U.N. supervision. He asked the United Nations to keep peacekeeping forces in Haiti for at least four more months. Although the U.N. troops had been scheduled to leave Haiti on July 31, Ambassador Richardson said, "What is needed is more time, four more months, so this very young police force can be better trained and mentored."

Ambassador Richardson also had the opportunity to draw upon his previous experience with Saddam Hussein. When United Nations leader Kofi Annan returned from Iraq with an agreement for inspections that would insure that Iraq was not stockpiling deadly weapons, Richardson cautioned, "Our concern is Saddam Hussein, and whether he will find loopholes in some of the ambiguities of the language." His own experience in negotiating with Hussein has given him invaluable insights into the way the Iraqi dictator's mind works.

The opportunities for making a difference as United States Ambassador to the United Nations

▼▼▼▼▼▼
Richardson asked the U.N. to keep peacekeeping forces in Haiti for at least four more months.
▲▲▲▲▲▲

Every technique he ever learned in a life of respecting different cultures and different viewpoints, he has brought to the negotiating table.

continued. Every technique he ever learned in a life of respecting different cultures and different viewpoints he has brought to the negotiating table. Bill Richardson demonstrated that he has the ability and determination to achieve his goals, and the goals of the nation.

As a result, President Clinton then nominated Richardson to become the United States' Secretary of Energy. In the remarks he made during his nomination speech on June 18, 1998, the president emphasized the many ways in which Bill Richardson has served his country, and the many abilities he brings to whatever role he is asked to play. President Clinton said, "Bill Richardson will do his part now to secure our energy future, at a time when it is inextricably bound up with our obligations as Americans for protection of the planet." On August 18, Bill Richardson was sworn in as the ninth United States Secretary of Energy following a unanimous confirmation by the U.S. Senate on July 31. He became the highest ranking Hispanic in the Clinton administration and the first New Mexican to serve as the Secretary of Energy. For a few weeks, he had to wear two hats: he was still U.N. Ambassador until the Senate confirmed his successor, and now he was also the energy secretary.

Whether Richardson will continue to use his abilities as a professional diplomat or whether he will return to elected office is a question only the future can answer. He has said that he would like to be either a governor or a senator for New Mexico, and he emphasizes, "I'm proud to be a politician. I like people. A politician basically is a persuader besides being a legislator; I like that part of the job."

BILL RICHARDSON

Whatever choices he makes, the recognition he has received in the past indicates how valuable his abilities and his efforts are. Bill Richardson has twice been nominated for the Nobel Peace Prize. He has received the Aztec Golden Eagle, the highest honor that Mexico awards to anyone not a Mexican citizen. He has made, and is continuing to make, a difference in thousands of lives all over the world.

54

LINDA CHAVEZ-THOMPSON

Labor Leader
1944–

"For me, as part of my duties and responsibilities, fighting every day for the rights of workers who don't have a voice, . . . that is the primary joy that I have, bringing a voice to people who oftentimes are not valued for their work and who oftentimes are not able to speak out for themselves.**"**

—Linda Chavez-Thompson as told to Valerie Menard, March 1998

BIO HIGHLIGHTS

- Born in Lorenzo, Texas, August 3, 1944; mother: Genoveva Ursua; father: Felipe Chavez
- At 12 years old, gave speech for Mexican Independence Day
- October 24, 1964, married Jose Luz Ramirez
- July 11, 1965, daughter, Maricela, was born
- December 7, 1967, hired as bilingual secretary for Laborer's Construction Local in Lubbock, Texas
- June 1971–July 1973, worked as international staff representative for the AFSCME
- Became executive director of AFSCME Local 2399
- June 21, 1976, son, Pedro, was born
- 1984, divorced Ramirez, but they remained good friends
- December 14, 1985, married Robert Thompson
- March 1995, became state director of AFSCME, Council 42
- October 25, 1995, elected executive vice president of the AFL-CIO, the first woman and first Latina to hold that position
- 1997, Appointed to President Clinton's Initiative on Race

Linda Chavez-Thompson

▼▼▼▼▼▼

One of Benito's favorite activities was local politics. He was a champion of the working men and women of Puerto Rico.

▲▲▲▲▲▲

American workers earn their pay every day, but they don't all work under the same conditions. Some employers appreciate the value of good employees and reward their staff with decent benefits, such as health insurance, retirement pay, vacation time and sick leave, or cash bonuses for a job well done. Other employers may not be so generous, which can create a stressful working environment. For employees working under these conditions, there's very little incentive to do a good job. Some workers join unions—organizations made up of workers in similar fields that deal directly with employers to improve conditions for its members. "Not all American workers are helpless," says Linda Chavez-Thompson, "only workers without a union."

To understand this comment, it is important to know that in 1995 Chavez-Thompson was elected executive vice president of one of the largest worker's unions in the country, the American Federation of Labor and Congress of Industrial Organizations (AFL-CIO). She considers her election one of the most memorable events in her life; for a woman who claims to have a true love and respect for the American worker, becoming the executive vice president of a labor union with a membership of 13 million does appear to be a dream come true. "My election as the executive vice president of the AFL-CIO is probably the highlight of my life and the reason is probably because I have become a symbol to many women and people of color who aspire to move up in their national and international unions. They see my election on October 25, 1995, as the beginning of change in the American labor movement."

LINDA CHAVEZ-THOMPSON

As the daughter of a cotton sharecropper, Chavez-Thompson gained her appreciation for workers early in life. She was born Lydia Chavez on August 3, 1944, in Lorenzo, Texas. Located in the western part of the state, Lorenzo is in an area where the majority of domestically produced cotton is grown. Lydia was the third oldest of eight children. She has four sisters—Maria, Martha, Janie, and Amy—and three brothers—Victor, Philip, and Tony. There are 21 years between the oldest in the family, Maria, and the youngest, Amy. It was Amy who gave Chavez-Thompson her first nickname, Lalo. Lalo is usually a nickname for Eduardo, but in this case it was baby Amy's way of pronouncing Lydia. Her first grade teacher thought the name Lydia was too exotic and opted to pronounce it Linda instead, a common experience among Hispanics.

At three years old— Linda on left

Chavez-Thompson's parents, Felipe Chavez and Genoveva Ursua, were first-generation Americans born in Texas. Their families had known each other in Mexico. Her father learned the farming trade from his father, Victor Chavez. According to Chavez-Thompson, "My father was a hard worker. He was dedicated to giving a good day's work, ten, fourteen hours a day." Her father may have been an example of a hard worker, but her mother demonstrated tremendous inner strength and wisdom. Felipe died in 1984; her mother lives in Austin, Texas.

Born in 1918, Genoveva was raised with old-fashioned ideas. Young women during that period were taught to obey their husbands and to never disagree with them. Even with that upbringing, says Chavez-Thompson, Genoveva never encouraged that kind of thinking in her daughters. "Despite all of her teaching and reservations, my mother never taught us that we could not be what we wanted to be. She never told us, as I'm sure her mother told her, 'You can't do this, you can't do that because they'll talk about you. They'll say that you want to be a man or worse.' She never scared us away from what we could be, and so I thought that I could do [anything]."

In small rural communities, there is usually just one school that everybody attends. In Lorenzo, Chavez-Thompson attended Lorenzo Elementary and Lorenzo Middle School. The family moved to another small town, Idalou, Texas, where Chavez-Thompson continued her middle school education at Idalou Middle School. She attended Idalou High School from 1959 to 1960.

Chavez-Thompson remembers learning very important lessons at a young age. When she was 10 years old, she got her first exposure to discrimination. She liked to draw, and her friends admired her drawings. She would draw clothes, and she and her friends would play fashion show with the drawings. They played together at school during recess and lunch. Then one day, her friends quit playing with her. They had been told by their mothers to stop playing with the

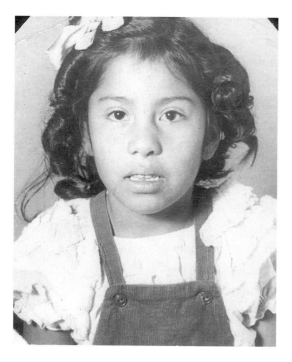

As a young girl, Linda learned about discrimination early in life.

"little Mexican girl." Chavez-Thompson says she was heartbroken. "I had never experienced this type of discrimination, and I somehow felt being 'Mexican' was dirty and shameful."

Chavez-Thompson looks back at another lasting impression that she carries with her in her work today. Her father demonstrated how important it was to be a hard worker, but she also saw how other workers, who were also hardworking, were mistreated on neighboring cotton farms. Unlike Chavez-Thompson, whose family lived and worked on the farm, these workers were migrants who traveled from town to town, working where they were needed. They were employed seasonally, harvesting crops. Once the harvest was done, they moved on. "They were U.S. citizens, but [they were] treated like third-class [citizens], and their living conditions were horrible," she says. The children of these migrant workers were ignored by the teachers because they knew they would only be in school for a few months and would not complete the term. "It bothered me," she says, "but as a child, I felt powerless to do anything other than to befriend them and have lunch with them when others in the school would not."

She also learned an important lesson from her grandfather, Victor. When she was 12 years old, she was asked to make a speech at a fiestas celebration for Mexican Independence Day, which is celebrated on September 16. Her grandfather made her practice the speech in front of him. He coached her how to speak slowly so that people could understand her and to use her hands and voice for emphasis. "I was the youngest speaker that evening, my speech was done all in

▼▼▼▼▼▼

"I had never experienced this type of discrimination, and I somehow felt being 'Mexican' was dirty and shameful."

▲▲▲▲▲▲

LINDA CHAVEZ-THOMPSON

Spanish, and my grandfather bragged about me for weeks," Chavez-Thompson remembers. "He told all within earshot that I was going to grow up to be like him, this despite the fact that he was old-fashioned about girls not being equal to boys."

Living on a cotton farm, Chavez-Thompson says she had little time for after-school activities. Besides the school bus in the morning, there was no transportation to take her into town or back home afterward. She does remember a physical education teacher in high school, Mr. Bramlett, who encouraged her to be more active in school by becoming involved in school government. "He praised my ability to memorize, to speak and articulate well, and said that my self-confidence showed. He repeatedly asked me to be the class monitor and made my high school freshman year very memorable."

She received a lot of encouragement to pursue her academic studies, but that wasn't enough to outweigh the financial difficulties facing her family. She quit high

Taken November 1970 in Dallas, Texas

school in her second year and began working instead. After a few years, she met and married her first husband, Jose Luz Ramirez, and on July 11, 1965, her daughter Maricela was born. (Eleven years later, she would have a second child, Pedro Javier, who was born June 21, 1976.) Two years after her daughter was born, she took a job as a bilingual secretary for a union, the Laborer's Construction Local, in Lubbock, Texas. What began for Chavez-Thompson as just a job would soon turn into a lifetime career.

Because her language skills in Spanish and English were so invaluable, Chavez-Thompson did not stay a secretary for long. She was asked to help out in other ways, and with each task she acquired more and more responsibilities. She began working directly with the union members. By working with the union hiring hall, she learned about workers' rights; and when she represented workers who had grievances or complaints with their employers, she learned how to deal with managers. She took a job with the Texas AFL-CIO, coordinating disaster relief efforts after a tornado hit the city on May 11, 1970. She helped union and nonunion families with housing, food, small business loan applications, and other needs.

Trained as a union organizer—someone who recruits new members and coordinates union activities—Chavez-Thompson became in September 1970 the first Latina hired in Texas as the laborers' district representative. She traveled through half the state organizing and representing Texas Laborers' Union and their issues to Texas senators, representatives, and the governor in the 1971 legislative session. Texas is considered an "at will" and a "right to

▼▼▼▼▼▼

By working with the union hiring hall, she learned about worker's rights.

▲▲▲▲▲▲

LINDA CHAVEZ-THOMPSON

Linda worked to get San Antonio mayor Henry Cisneros elected.

work" state, which gives much more power to employers, who can hire and fire employees at will. This also made Chavez-Thompson's work harder when she tried to change state laws to protect workers.

The family moved to Austin when she was hired as the international staff representative for the American Federation of State, County and Municipal Employees (AFSCME). She held this position from June 1971 to July 1973. She traveled extensively, organizing public employees throughout the state who worked for hospitals; city, state, and county government; and school districts. But because her job demanded so much time and her daughter was seeing less and less of her mother, Chavez-Thompson gave up her position as international representative and took a cut in pay. The family moved to San Antonio, where she took a job at a small union that she had helped organize.

Although it seemed she had taken a step backward in her career, her time spent with the smaller AFSCME local in San Antonio gave her the complete union experience. Chavez-Thompson was not limited by a title or job description; she did what needed to be done for the local. "I had to prepare grievances and present them. I had to argue against district attorneys and city attorneys who might present arguments against the members," she asserts. "I had to not only become more political, I had to get people elected." For government employees, the fastest way to improve their working conditions is to elect candidates who are sensitive to their needs. Chavez-Thompson worked to get San Antonio mayor Henry Cisneros elected and also to change the method of city council from an at-

LINDA CHAVEZ-THOMPSON

large to a single-member district election. *At-large* means the entire city votes for every position on the city council. With single-member districts, the city council is separated into districts, and each council person is elected to represent a district and not the entire city.

At AFSCME, Chavez-Thompson says she worked her way up through the ranks, starting as an assistant business manager, then business manager, and eventually to executive director of AFSCME Local 2399

October 1979—taken on the steps of City Hall in San Antonio, Texas

in late 1973. She held that position until February 1995. About her success, Chavez-Thompson says, "I brought with me a quick mind and a heart that was full of love for working people and gave it everything I had and built my reputation. When I dealt with management, I was always frank and honest. I would beat them up on an issue but I was respectful of the job they had to do and I think I deserved and got the respect from representing workers who oftentimes had a limited education like

mine. I had a talent for being able to speak and being eloquent in my representation of workers and people listened to me."

While her career was taking off, Chavez-Thompson suffered some personal setbacks. After 20 years, she and her husband realized that besides their two children, they had very little in common and that their marriage was over. She explains that the divorce was amicable. Both she and her husband wanted to maintain a friendly relationship for their children's sakes, but they also still felt friendly toward each other. "Neither one of us wanted to hurt our children. He and I both agreed the divorce was between us and had nothing to do with the kids." They are still good friends today.

Through her work, she met Robert Thompson, who worked with the Amalgamated Transit Union. Because both of them represented public employees with their respective unions—Chavez-Thompson was still working with AFSCME at the time—they found themselves working together on many of the same issues. They began dating after she divorced, and two years later, in 1985, they were married. Chavez-Thompson credits her second husband with much of her success at the AFL-CIO, including her election as executive vice president. "He was very supportive," she says, "very much the person who helped me get to where I am today."

There's an old saying that behind every successful man is a woman, which means that a man's ability to succeed depends on the support he receives from his wife. The same is true for Chavez-Thompson, only in reverse. Two years into their marriage, Robert

▼▼▼▼▼

Linda credits her second husband with much of her success at the AFL-CIO. He was very supportive.

▲▲▲▲▲▲

Thompson was offered a job with his union that would have required him to travel three weeks out of the month and which would have taken his career in a different direction than his wife's. He declined the offer. He told his wife that there was going to be only one politician in the family and that it was going to be her. "He gave up being his own politician in his union so that I could run for office [with AFSCME], which I did in 1988 and won. He was there for me at a time when I was going on the national scene in the labor movement, and he decided my going on to the national scene was the important piece of our partnership." She describes her seven-year marriage to Thompson as "wonderful." Unfortunately, in 1993, he died of lung cancer.

She left her position as executive director of AFSCME Local 2399 in February 1995 to work as the Texas state director of AFSCME Council 42. There she supervised statewide organizing efforts for the union and the legislative and political efforts for the union's 15,000 members from 25 locals. These efforts caught the attention of John Sweeney, a candidate for the position of the national president of the AFL-CIO. On May 31, 1995, Chavez-Thompson was invited by AFSCME International President McEntee, Sweeney and Richard Trumka to run on a slate with them as the executive vice president of the AFL-CIO. The decision to include Linda as the first woman and first Latina to hold such a high office in the AFL-CIO was deliberate and long overdue. "John Sweeney and Richard Trumka made a specific decision that there must be a change in the labor movement, and one of the ways to show people the change would be not only

▼▼▼▼▼▼

In May 1995, Linda was invited to run for executive vice president of the AFL-CIO.

▲▲▲▲▲▲

LINDA CHAVEZ-THOMPSON

to create a new position, but to make a deliberate attempt at putting someone that didn't look like the 'male and pale' description of the labor movement of old. That's when someone said, 'Okay, we have to look for a person of color and if at all possible a woman' and since I qualified on both counts and had certainly the credentials and qualification of over 28 years in the labor movement, they asked me."

The year Chavez-Thompson took office as executive vice president of the AFL-CIO followed a decade of what many in the labor movement refer to as the worst for organized labor. This horrible decade began back in 1981 when the Professional Air Traffic Controllers Organization (PATCO) went on strike,

Linda celebrated the election results at the annual AFL-CIO convention in New York on October 24, 1995

demanding better wages and benefits for their workers. Air traffic controllers work in airport towers, monitoring the position of airplanes in the sky to avoid midair collisions. They also clear airplanes for takeoffs and landings. Because of this awesome responsibility, their jobs have been rated the most stressful. According to the National Air Traffic Controllers Association (NATCA), air traffic controllers safely direct more than 60 million aircraft annually to their destinations.

Air traffic is controlled by the Federal Aviation Administration, which makes air traffic controllers government employees. When they staged a strike (refused to work) in 1981, they struck against the U.S. government. Rather than negotiate with them, President Ronald Reagan fired 11,400 controllers and decertified their union, PATCO. This action sent a message nationwide that no worker was protected, not even by a union. It wasn't until 1987 that air traffic controllers were allowed to elect a new union, NATCA.

According to Chavez-Thompson, what happened to the air traffic controllers struck a horrible blow to the labor movement that could have been avoided. Labor leaders didn't react, she says, they just kept waiting for Reagan to get out of office and be replaced by a Democratic president. Instead, Reagan was reelected.

Union members tend to vote with the Democratic Party, and Democratic candidates tend to support the issues of labor. However, Bill Clinton, a Democratic president, signed the North American Free Trade Agreement (NAFTA) in 1994. Organized labor opposed the agreement, arguing that NAFTA would send jobs away from the U.S. and into Mexico and

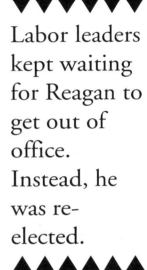

▼▼▼▼▼▼
Labor leaders kept waiting for Reagan to get out of office. Instead, he was re-elected.
▲▲▲▲▲▲

LINDA CHAVEZ-THOMPSON

▼▼▼▼▼▼

"The labor movement finally woke up in 1994. We were waiting for a Democratic president to come save us. Finally, we realized we'd better save ourselves."

▲▲▲▲▲▲

Canada. "The labor movement, to some extent, finally woke up in 1994," Chavez-Thompson explains. "We had been sitting around for fourteen years, [waiting for] a Democratic president [to] come and save us. [We realized] we better save ourselves and that's when our slate ran for office in 1995."

The AFL-CIO was formed in 1955 with the merger of a group of craft unions and an alliance of industrial unions. Today, 78 autonomous unions can be found under the AFL-CIO banner. Its union members include the Teamsters, AFSCME, the Service Employees International Union, the United Farm Workers (UFW), and the United Food and Commercial Workers. When the United Parcel Service workers struck in 1997, the AFL-CIO supported them. However, unions support the American worker in other ways than during strikes. According to Chavez-Thompson, one of her immediate concerns is to correct the unequal pay women receive as compared to men. "Women earn 74 cents on the dollar of what men earn for comparable jobs," she says. "We've been talking about equal pay for years, and I want to do something about it."

But the most important goal of the union is to protect a worker's right to form a union. According to the Bureau of Labor Statistics, workers who join unions make 33 percent more money. For people of color, that percentage is even greater. Wages for African American union workers are 42 percent greater than the wages of African American nonunion workers. Latinos earn 52 percent more if they join a union. Job security is also greater for union workers. According to an AFL-CIO analysis, 60 percent of union members have held a job for a least ten years, while only 32.6 percent of nonunion workers have managed to stay at the same job for that long.

In September 1997, Chavez-Thompson led an AFL-CIO women's march.

It's not hard to understand why a worker would want to join a union, but it's also easy to see why a company would resist efforts to organize its employees. "Having the right to organize is the same in this country as the right to a fair trial or the civil rights that protect us from discrimination," explains Chavez-Thompson. "We believe it is a civil right, it is a given right for people to be free from intimidation and harassment for trying to join a union or bring a union into the workplace."

LINDA CHAVEZ-THOMPSON

Besides men like Sweeney and her late husband, Chavez-Thompson admits to two other role models in the labor movement: Cesar Chavez and Rosa Walker. Chavez, who founded the United Farm Workers (UFW), impressed her with his humility and dedication. Like the cotton pickers Chavez-Thompson remembers as a girl, farmworkers have always been vulnerable to mistreatment. When Cesar Chavez saw

these people and the conditions in which they worked and lived, he decided that only if they united could they demand better wages and living conditions. But because farmworkers are some of the poorest-paid workers, they couldn't afford huge union fees. As a result, the UFW had little money to invest in campaigns and lobbies for their members. Instead, the UFW would call for boycotts (refusal to purchase) of certain foods to force growers to improve the situation of the workers.

"Cesar Chavez was definitely a role model for me. He represented the people who earn even less than minimum wage workers because they might have to work six, seven months out of the year and that kind of union is really based more on faith and hope than anything else," says Chavez-Thompson.

Rosa Walker influenced Chavez-Thompson because she was one of highest-ranking women in the Texas AFL-CIO. "She put wonderful programs together for the state federation in Texas. These [Chavez and Walker] are the two primary people that I looked at making a difference in the world of labor and politics."

The time spent away from her family is still what bothers her most about her job. Her son works in the offices of the Service Employees International Union as a mail clerk, but her daughter, who works as a transportation inspector for the city of San Antonio, is married and has two children (a son named Jose Felipe and a daughter named Lydia). Chavez-Thompson travels so extensively that she's even developed a taste for airline food. "Being away from my daughter and my grandchildren I guess is probably

▼▼▼▼▼▼
"Cesar Chavez was definitely a role model for me. He represented workers who earn even less than minimum wage..."
▲▲▲▲▲▲

the worst part. I don't get to see them grow up, I don't get to be with them as often as I would like to be."

Once she is on the road, she experiences one of her favorite aspects of the job: meeting union members. From her office in Washington, D.C., Chavez-Thompson can issue memos to AFL-CIO members, advising them about organizing efforts or how to participate in different programs offered by the union. But she has found that meeting the union's constituents in person is much more inspiring, for them and for her. "Meeting thousands of union

At a White House news conference on equal pay legislation: left to right: Linda Chavez-Thompson, Senator Edward Kennedy, Eunice Shriver, and Congressman Patrick Kennedy.

LINDA CHAVEZ-THOMPSON

members and inspiring them to do their job but also to make a greater effort in the community they live in to make sure the labor story gets told as many times and to as many people as possible—I enjoy that part of it the most," she says. "For me, as part of my duties and responsibilities, fighting every day for the rights of workers who don't have a voice, for me that is the primary joy that I have, bringing a voice to people who oftentimes are not valued for their work and who oftentimes are not able to speak out for themselves."

This kind of dedication and hard work has not been ignored. Chavez-Thompson has received numerous awards, including honorary doctorates from

Linda attended the inaugural reception at Vice President Al Gore's home. Left to right: V.P. Al Gore, Chavez-Thompson, Mike Croshaw, and Tipper Gore.

LINDA CHAVEZ-THOMPSON

President Clinton appointed Linda to the President's Race Advisory Board. On September 30, 1997, President Clinton addressed a meeting of the board at a Washington hotel.

several colleges such as Mount Holyoke, Princeton University, and Wesleyan University. Most recently, she was honored with a presidential appointment to President Clinton's Initiative on Race. Aware of the growing race problems in the U.S., in February 1997 Clinton appointed a nine-member panel and charged them with conducting town meetings nationwide in an attempt to research the causes and solutions to racial problems. Based on the board's early reports, the president has already begun a program called High Hopes, which matches a college student with a junior high school student for tutoring and mentoring. The program is aimed at reducing the high-school dropout rate.

Linda Chavez-Thompson

There will be more reports, including one final report in 1998. "The work of the initiative has been absolutely phenomenal," asserts Chavez-Thompson. "We have worked very extensively in trying to identify problems of race such as poverty, stereotyping, workplace discrimination, and the justice system's effect on minority youth." But when it comes to redefining race as more than a "black and white" issue, Chavez-Thompson admits that as the only Latino on the board, her work is cut out for her. "It is very hard to do although I have tried to make some headway. The press has not been helpful. They do not lend as much attention to the fact that there are other people of color out there besides blacks and that there are other issues. But yes, Latinos do have a story to tell."

Her future plans revolve around the union. She loves her job and hopes to continue in her position as executive vice president. The AFL-CIO brought in 400,000 new members in 1997, the first year in a long while that the union did not experience a major loss in its membership. Organized labor is making a comeback, which means that entering the next century, American workers will be less vulnerable, and Linda Chavez-Thompson's job might get a little easier.

▼▼▼▼▼▼

Linda's future plans revolve around the union. She loves her job and hopes to continue in her position as executive vice president.

▲▲▲▲▲▲

CARLOS MENCIA

Comedian
1967–

"**N**o matter how many times you hear people say, 'You are the future,' believe it because you are. But you need to take that responsibility and make sure you make the world a better place for the children of the future who will follow you. "

—Carlos Mencia, as told to Valerie Menard, February 1998

BIO HIGHLIGHTS

- Born Ned Mencia on October 22, 1967, in Honduras; mother: Magdalena Mejia; father: Roberto Holness; raised by uncle Juan Pablo Mejia and his wife, Consuelo Aguilar, in East Los Angeles
- At age 13, taken out of school and sent to work on a family ranch in Honduras
- Three years later, returned to Los Angeles to go to high school
- 1985–1988, studied electrical engineering at California State College, Los Angeles
- 1988, took a coworker's advice and performed a comedy routine for the first time
- 1989, won first place on Star Search in Spanish, televised on the Univision network
- 1993, appeared on Arsenio Hall and received a standing ovation
- 1994, hosted *Loco Slam* on HBO and starred in one episode of the series *HBO Comedy Half Hour*
- 1995, featured in a second *HBO Comedy Half Hour,* which was nominated for a Cable Ace Award
- 1997, performed in the Latino Laugh Festival
- 1998, debuted as the host of the English language show, *Funny Is Funny,* on the Spanish-language network Galavision

Carlos Mencia

Growing up in East Los Angeles, the second youngest of 16 brothers and sisters, Carlos Mencia had a unique perspective on life. Given his natural competitive nature, it wasn't too surprising that he would succeed at whatever he decided to do, but how he succeeded was also important. He could have been financially successful as an electrical engineer, which he was studying to be in college, but instead he chose to make people laugh and became a comedian. "I think we all feel the same things most of the time, we just don't know how to put it into words," Mencia explains. "When I'm onstage, I say it. The truth makes people laugh."

Menica was born in Honduras on October 22, 1967, and originally named Ned; but from that moment, his life would be unlike most children's. His birth parents, Magdalena Mejia and Roberto Holness, both from Honduras, decided to give their youngest child at the time to Magdalena's brother, Juan Pablo Mejia and his wife, Consuelo Aguilar (who was from Zacatecas, Mexico), to raise. His Uncle Pablo and Aunt Consuelo could not have children of their own. Ned wasn't totally removed from his family, however; he grew up in East Los Angeles next door to his siblings: Santos, Juaquin, Manuel, Anna, Marta, Maribel, Olga, Dysis, Josel, Jenny, Cristina, Dorca, Rosa, Loreli, and Albert. He also has two half-brothers on his father's side, Roberto and Juan. Nevertheless, he feels that his true parents are Consuelo and Juan Pablo. He eventually took his grandmother's maiden name, Mencia and changed his first name to Carlos. He went from Ned to Carlos in 1988 when he began working at the Comedy Store. The owner, Mitzi Shore, encouraged him to change his name. He chose Carlos.

His adoptive parents met in the United States at a school where they were taking English classes. They had both just emigrated—his mother from Mexico, his father from Honduras—and were still teenagers. His father worked at several jobs, but usually as a construction worker and engineer, and consequently earned the nickname Pablo Gump from his children. Consuelo earned a beautician's license and became a hairdresser in Hollywood, California. Working in Hollywood, she eventually developed a client list that included at least one celebrity that Mencia can remember, the actor Tony Curtis.

This school picture was taken of Carlos when he was in Honduras.

CARLOS MENCIA

Carlos attended Hammel Street School in East Los Angeles from pre-kindergarten to sixth grade. Immediately, he demonstrated exceptional intelligence in school. For Mencia, making good grades "was easy," almost to the point of being boring. Unlike most comedians, he wasn't the class clown in school; he was the opposite. "I was never a funny guy," Mencia tells Chuck Crisafulli in a 1994 *Los Angeles Times* interview. "I was never the guy cracking jokes at school. I was the kid in the back of the classroom who shut up and did his work. Half the students didn't know who I was, and the other half hated me for ruining the grading curve."

Pablo and Consuelo Mejia taken during a visit to Los Angeles in 1998.

For that reason, he can't say which subject at school interested him the most, because they all seemed the same. Students with that kind of experience in school have been analyzed as having a photographic memory, which means their minds work like a camera. They remember everything they read, practically word for word, after reading it only once. Mencia isn't sure, but he thinks he may be blessed with that gift.

School days tended to be fairly unmemorable, continues Carlos, but when he thinks back to his time in elementary school, he does remember what he calls a "defining moment." One of his classmates at the

CARLOS MENCIA

Hammel Street School had only one leg. Anything that makes kids different in school can be traumatic, but for disabled children, they can't hide what makes them different. They live with it every day. Other children treat disabled kids in good and bad ways: some ignore it, some don't. Disabled kids cope with this in good and bad ways, too. This classmate, says Carlos, used anger as his defense mechanism. He happened to pick a fight with a girl on the playground and took off his prosthetic (fake) leg and swung it at her. Carlos intervened, grabbed the leg, and hit the boy with it. "If he hadn't been so mean, I would have defended him," asserts Carlos, "but just because he had a handicap didn't give him a license to be a bully. That day taught me that I have the ability to treat people the same, regardless."

Carlos entered middle school, where he attended classes for gifted students. The teachers suggested he skip grades seven, eight, and nine, moving from sixth to tenth grade. Skipping grades places extremely intelligent students in classes that are challenging. But there can also be a negative impact. Students who skip grades, especially in high school, will interact with students who are older instead of with their peers. Mencia's parents worried that at 13 years old, Carlos would be exposed to students three years older than he was and that he might get involved in things he shouldn't be at such a young age. Instead, they decided to take Carlos out of school and send him to live and work on a ranch in Sico, Honduras, with his adoptive father.

It's not hard to imagine how a young boy feels, leaving the rest of his family and going to a new

Carlos entered middle school, where he attended classes for gifted students. Teachers suggested he skip from grade six to ten.

▼▼▼▼▼▼

Carlos was born in Honduras to Honduran parents, but the kids in Honduras laughed at him.

▲▲▲▲▲▲

country, and not attending school but working. He went from city life in sunny California to life on a farm that was surrounded by a jungle. It wasn't easy, especially for someone who was used to excelling. He took up carving, learned how to milk cows, ride horses, and speak Spanish fluently. He also began playing soccer when he was in Honduras. He continued playing in high school back in the U.S. and had offers to play professionally later on. He opted instead, to attend college.

At first, the kids in Honduras laughed at him. But his natural competitive spirit kicked in, and by the end of three years, he had mastered every skill, especially horseback riding. He also learned that Latinos outside of the United States had a very different attitude toward Latinos in the United States. Although he was born in Honduras to Honduran parents, he had been raised in the United States by a Mexican mother and a Honduran father, which made his identity unclear in Honduras and even more uncertain when he did return to the United States. His parent kept him in Honduras for three years, long enough for him to return to school as a tenth-grader, the same grade he would have been in had his parents allowed him to skip. "I'm more than Honduran, than Mexican or Mexican American," Mencia says. "I'm even more than just American, but being that I live here in the U.S., I'm comfortable with being called anything, but the acknowledgment of the fact that I am American, to me, is extremely important."

Back in Los Angeles, Carlos attended Garfield High School. Even though he had been out of school for three years, he immediately picked up where he left off. He did have to deal with the culture shock of coming from another country, which made it difficult to make new friends. "I was so used to being alone, learning how to be by myself. But it hurt my social skills a little and I found it hard to make friends. In high school everybody seemed different than I was." There was one teacher, Mr. Benson, who taught anthropology and government, who Mencia remembers inspired him to be creative. "He was the coolest teacher. He really encouraged me to be successful at whatever I decided to do." Mencia graduated from Garfield in 1985 and enrolled in California State University, Los Angeles, where he began studying electrical engineering.

At brother Albert's wedding: from left: Sisters Olga and Martha, mother Magdalena, Carlos, and sister Dysis

While at Cal State L.A., he worked at Farmer's Insurance in the printing department. He worked during the day and went to school at night, from 5:00 P.M. to 10:00 P.M. When he got home he would stay up and watch the popular talk shows at the time. "When I got home I watched Arsenio Hall and Joan Rivers. I was so enthralled by these guys telling jokes that I would go to work the next day and tell the

jokes with such enthusiasm that people thought I was funny." He remembers standing around the water cooler with his fellow workers and making them laugh.

CARLOS MENCIA

Neither the job nor his schoolwork held much interest for Mencia, so it's not surprising that when a coworker suggested he do stand-up comedy, he took it seriously. "I knew I wasn't going to do anything with what I knew [about electrical engineer or printing]." It also helped that the company was planning to relocate and Mencia didn't want to go. He took a leave of absence from work instead.

Before taking the advice, Mencia started going to comedy clubs just to see what they were like and to watch other comics. In a 1994 interview in *Hispanic* magazine, Mencia describes his thoughts: "I had an amazing time. I never laughed so much as I did that night. As I moved with the crowd toward the exit, I stopped and looked back toward stage. A little voice in my head told me I could get onstage and make people laugh." He decided to sign up to perform at an open-mike amateur night at a comedy club in Los Angeles called the Laugh Factory. When he first got onstage, it didn't look promising. Three minutes into the routine, he drew a blank, admitted it to the audience, and walked off the stage. The audience loved it and the owner, who thought Mencia had done that as part of his routine, told him never to stop doing comedy. From that moment, he says, "I didn't choose comedy, it chose me." One month later, Mencia performed at another club called the Comedy Store and was so successful that the owners asked him to continue performing every night. This was the end of his college career, which had lasted from 1985 to 1988, and the beginning of a whole new life for him.

Many comedians have said that to make an audience laugh is addictive, almost like taking a drug.

▼▼▼▼▼
"I didn't choose comedy," says Carlos. "It chose me."
▲▲▲▲▲

84

Performing at the Comedy Store in Los Angeles

Most of us have experienced something like that. Even among friends, we know that if we tell a joke and our friends laugh, we immediately try to tell another to make them laugh again. As Mencia puts it, "As soon

CARLOS MENCIA

as I saw I could get people to laugh, I wanted to be as funny as humanly possible." However, for a comedian to make people laugh, it takes a lot of skill. Timing—when you deliver the punch line—and how you tell a

Performing at the HBO Comedy Half Hour

joke has been called an art form. For the first two years of his new career, he traveled to comedy clubs and restaurants throughout Los Angeles to appear on amateur nights. Mencia noted other comics and how they performed. "I watched 20 to 30 comedians perform each night. I watched how they worked and how they got the audience on their side. I studied why some comedians did better earlier or later in the evening," he says.

It's also important for comedians to develop a style that makes them unique. As a Latino, Mencia was already different from most comedians, but he also had to develop his own style. That style was urban and angry.

CARLOS MENCIA

He was inspired by such comics as Richard Pryor and Sam Kinison. Both men included social commentary, and both men showed differing degrees of anger in their comedy act. Pryor used saber-sharp sarcasm to express his anger, while Kinison just yelled. Mencia combines the two, using sarcasm at times and yelling at others. "If you take some of the most prominent performers of all time, they were minorities or misunderstood, very passionate, and sometimes boisterous, loud people. People like Pryor, Sam Kinison, Lenny Bruce, and George Carlin, who were like outlaw comics, supposedly—that's what comedy is. It's our job to reflect upon things that other people don't. Even if I'm saying things in an angry way, it speaks to the anger in everybody."

When he's described as urban, that means his jokes usually refer to his experience growing up in a big city like Los Angeles. For example, after the Los Angeles riots in 1992, Mencia started telling jokes about what he saw. During the riot, he jokes, "Blacks were all mad at Mexicans. Just because we looted better. My dad was like a quarterback in Kmart: 'All right, I got aisle seven. Mijo (son), you get the Pampers. Ready, break.'"

He also chose to take a "blue" rather than "clean" approach. In comedy, a comedian who works blue talks a lot and in detail about sex and uses profanity fairly regularly. A clean comic, like Jerry Seinfeld or Bill Cosby, rarely curses or talks in great detail about sex. In the beginning, Mencia's technique seemed to get more recognition than the comedy. He's been asked to explain his choice of technique so many times that now, he says, he's beginning to get offended.

▼▼▼▼▼▼
Carlos was inspired by such comics as Richard Pryor and Sam Kinison.
▲▲▲▲▲▲

CARLOS MENCIA

As a rising star, Carlos hosted the Friday late-night series **Loco Slam** on HBO.

No one questions comics like Seinfeld or Tim Allen, says Mencia. Critics come to his show just to count how many times he curses: "They don't hear the message underneath the joke." His only objective is to make people laugh, and if he does that, where's the problem? "I'm funny. My job on stage is to make people laugh. What I do on stage only serves one purpose and one alone, to make people laugh. My material has context to it, and because of the context of my material, at times, it seems like I'm angry, but it's just passion and it's part of the show."

After winning first place on Star Search in Spanish on the Univision network, Mencia began to get noticed by television executives and in 1994 was asked to host a show on Home Box Office (HBO) called *Loco Slam.* It was modeled after the *Russell Simmons Def Comedy Jam,* a comedy showcase featuring African American comics, which was also on

HBO. *Loco Slam* featured Latino artists. After that show, HBO offered Mencia another television spot as one of the featured comics in the series *HBO Comedy Half Hour.*

Mencia has continued to build his career on each new opportunity. Comedians spend most of their careers on the road, performing at comedy clubs across the country. The more they perform, the greater the chance that they'll get opportunities on television. After each stint in television, Mencia keeps his career momentum going by getting back on the road.

He was scheduled to be in a television sitcom called *Carlos,* but it never aired. Mencia kept touring and performing on HBO. He became part of a new wave of Latino comics who began to get noticed by American audiences. Besides the shows on HBO, programs like *Comedy Compadres,* which was produced by former comedy club owner and stand-up comic Jeff Valdez, also helped. Mencia eventually performed on *Comedy Compadres,* and his association with Valdez would eventually profit both men. "When I hosted a TV show called *Comedy Compadres* in Los Angeles, that somewhat began the Latino surge in comedy," Mencia asserts. "Before that, that wasn't the case. Before that, we knew Paul Rodriguez, he was our army of Latino comedy. I mean, we knew [of] nobody but him."

Comedy clubs in Los Angeles such as the Improv and the Comedy Store also began to feature Latino comedy nights. Although it was great to see Latino comics gaining momentum, Mencia says Latino comics need to be careful to not get stereotyped by writing all their jokes for one type of audience. "I think

▼▼▼▼▼

Mencia has continued to build his career on each new opportunity.
▲▲▲▲▲▲

Mencia works hard to have an act that can be understood by anyone but still includes his Latino culture.

young comics are stuck, somewhat. If you perform in Los Angeles, at all the Latino nights, what's going to happen? These guys [comics] are going to use a lot of ethnic references, like throwing words in there that nobody understands but Mexicans, and then what happens is somebody is going to see him and say, 'You know, he's really funny, but I can't book him in Tulsa [Oklahoma].' There's 50 states; California and Texas only make up two."

Mencia has worked hard to have an act that can be understood by anyone but still includes his Latino culture. He doesn't prefer one type of audience to another, but he sees the value in both. After all, he asks, "What's more important, to teach our own people that we can be successful or to teach the majority of America that we can be successful? I don't know, but I do know this. My people know me. They understand me. Even if they don't like how I say things, they understand me. I think that a lot of America doesn't understand that we've been emigrating into this country for so long and that we're not all new immigrants who just crossed the border."

As a good businessman, Mencia also appreciates the value of his Latino fan base and never takes it for granted. In Austin, Texas, Mencia was booked to perform two shows a night on Cinco de Mayo weekend, with another Latino comic, Jeff Garcia, opening the show. Although the gig wasn't for an official Latino night, Mencia believes it was no coincidence that the club booked Latinos on that weekend. When he arrived, he asked the club manager how many tickets had been sold. The shows hadn't sold out, but the manager assured him that the club rarely did sell out. Sensing that the club manager had not made an effort to promote the show to Latinos, Mencia immediately contacted the local Tejano stations and set up interviews so that he could promote the show himself. Almost immediately after the radio show, ticket sales soared. Every show sold out.

Latino nights at comedy clubs do sometimes give new comedians a chance to perform, and in one instance the concept was expanded into a festival. Valdez returned to the scene in 1996 when he introduced the Latino Laugh Festival. It featured unknown and established Latino comics, short films, and comedy sketches. Broadcast on the cable network Showtime, the show was so successful the first year, it was renewed for a second year. In 1997, Valdez asked Mencia to perform, but he stipulated that Mencia try to do a clean act. Mencia complied, and working

With girlfriend Amy Lyda

together again prompted Valdez to offer Mencia a chance at another television show, this time to be broadcast on the Spanish-language network Galavision. Galavision is the leading Hispanic cable network in the United States, currently available in more than 7.5 million homes.

Latino television programming on mainstream networks has not been very successful.

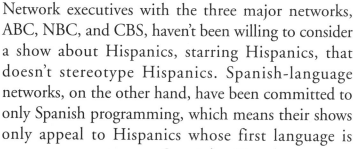

CARLOS MENCIA

Two new shows were launched on Galavision in 1998: *Café Olé with Giselle Fernandez* and *Funny is Funny* hosted by Mencia.

Network executives with the three major networks, ABC, NBC, and CBS, haven't been willing to consider a show about Hispanics, starring Hispanics, that doesn't stereotype Hispanics. Spanish-language networks, on the other hand, have been committed to only Spanish programming, which means their shows only appeal to Hispanics whose first language is Spanish. However, many Hispanics speak English and watch mainstream television, so Valdez decided to try a new approach—create English programming for Spanish-language networks.

Valdez formed a new company, Sí TV, and launched two shows on Galavision: *Cafe Olé with Giselle Fernandez* and *Funny Is Funny,* hosted by Mencia. *Funny Is Funny* is a half-hour comedy show featuring Latino comics. According to Galavision director of marketing, Michelle Bella, "By offering a bilingual programming block, Galavision will now tap into the English-speaking bilingual Hispanics who encompass the remainder of the U.S. Hispanic family." For Mencia, this type of programming was long overdue: "Many of us [who were born and educated here] get lumped in with Teodoro who just crossed the border and watches Telemundo and Univision and they think our dollars are gonna be spent in America through those venues and that is not the case."

The first season of *Funny Is Funny* was such a success that Galavision has renewed it for a second year. Mencia has other projects he plans to complete as well: a comedy album, a television show for an English-language network, and a children's cartoon. The album, which will be called *Judge Carlos*, was recorded as a live album three years ago, but the record company has yet to distribute it. Carlos distributes tapes and CDs at his own shows. Creating a television sitcom with Hispanics is also an ultimate goal for Mencia. "It's something that I'm definitely going to do, and the Latino community, America, needs to see a Latin actor/comedian/performer being a star on a sitcom. I feel like I need to do that, you know. I need to put my efforts into making our society a better one," he says in an interview with Vincent Lopez for *Grimmoires*.

Even though he has plans for television, these projects won't keep him from doing stand-up. "I'll always be onstage, one way or another." When he's not touring, he entertains himself by going to the movies and building and flying remote-control planes. He also enjoys jet-skiing, motorcycles, and plain relaxing. He hopes to earn a pilot's license soon so that he can fly his own plane someday. He goes to Honduras whenever he gets a chance.

Life, says Mencia, should be enjoyed. "Some people always see a negative. Not me. I can always find something positive in anything." Even when he looks back at his childhood and how he had to deal with

▼▼▼▼▼

The first season of *Funny is Funny* was such a success that Galavision renewed it for a second year.

▲▲▲▲▲▲

challenges many other kids didn't face, he can find many happy moments. Mencia credits his parents as his heroes. Their love and support has helped him to be successful. He recalls one Christmas when he was

Carlos (seated center) enjoyed his 30th birthday party with friends.

14 that captures the kind of relationship he shared with his parents. Mencia had fallen asleep in front of the Christmas tree. He heard his father come into the room, but he pretended to still be asleep. His father kissed him on the cheek and said, "I love you. You're my reason for living."

His parents' love came first, but Mencia also believes that to be successful, you must have goals, and the only way they can be achieved is through hard work. "Success," he says, "is all about work. You have to be willing to put in the time it takes to be successful." He also encourages kids to "be the best you can be. If you do that, opportunities will come your way." But the most important thing for children to believe, he says, is that they are the future. "No matter how many times you hear people say, 'You are the future,' believe it because you are. But you need to take that responsibility and make sure you make the world a better place for the children of the future who will follow you."

With his success in comedy and television, Carlos Mencia has apparently taken his own advice.